Sanitarium Magazine
Issue no. 31

*Thank you to all of our contributors,
we couldn't have done it without you.*

Contents

Dear Reader,

As the darkness of winter recedes and we edge towards spring, horror is creeping slowly out from the shadows and towards the fresh new dawn. This, my friends is a good thing, in my mind anyway. Studios with pedigree and backing behind them are optioning horror novels and the authors are having their say in Hollywood.

The 80's and 90's were a great time for horror and I personally believe this is coming back around. More and more horror stories, graphic novels and screenplays are being created and more importantly – championed by true fans of the industry.

With all this organic growth it is a great time to be a horror fan. And the team at Sanitarium are set to bring you the best new writers, artists and macabre news each and every month. We are also casting our net a little further and will be interviewing directors / filmmakers in the coming months, so if you need a little "downtime" from all that reading – we have your back.

Welcome to the Sanitarium

Barry Skelhorn

S
The Peculiar Death Of Barnabas Crackle
Brooke Warra
Physician: Dr. Roundtree
8245-AVD12
#59533

Barnabas Crackle died much as he had lived, strangely and alone.

He lay jittering and gasping in his final moments, ass-over-tea-kettle with his red stockinged feet pointing at the popcorn ceiling of his single-wide trailer, and a headset squawking in his ear. In the end it was the thing he loved the most that killed him so thoroughly.

The day had begun like any other ordinary day for Barnabas Crackle. That is to say, as extra-ordinarily as his days typically began, which were the usual for our faithful protagonist. He'd opened his eyes at precisely 7 a.m. for his first shift on the phone lines according to his body's own rhythm, risen from his futon, and padded into the closet-sized bathroom for a record-breaking piss. He'd smoked exactly two long-stemmed clove cigarettes while he donned his fake eyelashes edged in glitter and a favorite pair of red pantyhose underneath his usual uniform of filthy blue sweatpants. He ground the ash into the carpet with his toes and plopped down at the multi-line phone for a day of work.

Nestled in his bulging 400-pound frame lay the sweet mannerisms and cherubic face of an angel. His purplish, glistening lips, caked with the powder from his crunchy snacks formed a delicate bow around every ruthless insult and wild perversion he spewed into the mic-end of his headset. One could almost say that when Barnabas Crackle swore it was like watching red demons slither out of the mouth of an angel. To his clients, he was the faceless Tanya. A bodiless, silky voice they paid 3.99 a minute to turn their darkest desires into a symphony of pants, whispers, and degrading commandments.

It was a small town. He saw the uncomfortable way the butcher avoided his eyes when he came in every Friday morning for his lamb chops. He could not ignore the way the sheriff repeatedly cleared his throat and attempted to lower his own voice when Barnabas had called about delinquent kids spray-painting malicious words on his trailer. See, the voice of Tanya was not an invention and her extension number could be found in various tavern lavatories. Often, business boomed after these real-life meetings. Their ardor was aflame after having secretly watched him sashay away out of the corner of their eyes, sometimes with their wives mindlessly standing near. Waddle is an unfair description of Barnabas Crackle's gait for the ample man truly seemed to float on his tiny feet. In an interview that was anonymously given to the local paper after his untimely death the source was quoted as having said he "was the most dignified person I ever had the pleasure of knowing."

It may be hard for some to reconcile the two accounts, this anonymous source's apparent admiration for such a character as Barnabas Crackle, poor dear soul who was known for the brilliant orange of his Cheeto-stained fingertips and his propensity for collecting the outdated Jubilation Julie dolls.

His mother, god-rest-her-soul, had started the collection during his childhood when Barnabas had first biologically failed to be a female baby but grew to be just as sweet and soft and lovely as any daughter she ever hoped to have. The two had lovingly, if not a little obsessively amassed the dolls, arranging, re-arranging, and dusting them together over the years. When Ms. Crackle (never married, not that it's any business of yours thank you very much) passed suddenly of a stroke in the parking lot of her church, Barnabas inherited the smoke-ridden trailer they'd always shared and the massive treasure of Jubilation Julie dolls. It was little consolation for losing one's best friend and confidant. One's only friend and confidant. However heartbroken, he vowed he'd finish the collection and so took up his calling as a sex-phone operator to pay for the rare dolls.

The instrument of his death had come to him a few weeks prior to this day, when he'd bought the very last of the Jubilation Julie dolls in existence from the sheriff's wife. He'd been invited to their home to see his purchase before agreements were made and as he left with the doll clutched under his arm he felt the intent gaze of the sheriff on his backside all the way down the driveway.

The doll was a depiction of Jubilation Julie as the threadbare Sad Clown. Her normally brunette ringlets were a garish blue, a grotesque red frown scribbled around her bowtie mouth, and instead of her usual all-American attire she wore a drooping man's suit. Barnabas sat her next to the other Jubilation Julie's on the shelf-the Independence Day, the First Day of School, the Confirmation, and the beloved Snow Day and all the others. To say this moment was anti-climactic for Barnabas Crackle is like saying that an ice-storm was a bit blustery. His grief was momentous in that instant, an unbearable, gut-wrenching force. Somewhere nearby the leaky kitchen faucet that had for-all-time dripped a steady flow of droplets night and day, began to chant "snap, snap, snap". And so, Barnabas Crackle did just that.

That was the day the dolls began to whisper to him.

When they found the body it was first noted and then promptly concealed that the sheriff had phoned in the distress call. He was standing outside Barnabas Crackle's single-wide with a handful of forgotten daisies he clutched ruthlessly in his hand, wearing a rumpled, ill-fitting sports jacket that he hadn't properly dusted off after pulling it from the back of his closet. When the paramedics rushed in they found our dear Barnabas Crackle tits-up, powdered porcelain and lead paint chips on his lips, smiling at the dimpled glass in his front door. It had taken him weeks to consume the entire collection of Jubilation Julie dolls and his final view had been of love's earnest face peering through his window.

The End.

Brooke Warra

Brooke Warra grew up and developed a deep fascination with the macabre in a fishing village in the Pacific Northwest with her very Finnish family. She writes and lives with her two children near Phoenix, Arizona. She has been previously published in Under The Bed Magazine and has a writing prompt ebook available on Amazon.

S
A Little Nest Egg
Kenneth C. Goldman
Physician: Dr. Peterson
8268-WCT29
#60869

THE OLD FARM HOUSE LAY HIDDEN BEHIND A
FORTRESS of neglected shrubbery, and had it not been for the
freckled brown and white cat, Willy McCorkle would have
sped right past it. The animal had darted out into the road from
nowhere and Willy never even saw it. He heard only the sharp
crunch of bones and the thick squoosh of innards as the animal
thumped beneath the front tire of the Ford pick-up and burst
open. The cat rolled a few yards like a small furry sack, then lay
soaking in its own thick gravy leaking its guts into the cracked
asphalt fifty yards behind him.

Willy noticed the weather-beaten old house peeking through
the thatch of bushes that separated it from the road and
wondered if perhaps inside some withered prune of a woman
would be expecting her tabby to be lapping up a dish of milk in
her kitchen right about now. The thought curled his lips into a
toothy smile. This was almost too easy.

Just weeks earlier Willy would have had little use for a
jerkwater town like Loomis Falls, excepting those times he had
pulled his truck off the Interstate to guzzle down a few cold
ones or to take a dump behind a tree. But six months of dipping
into the cash receipts at Al Kelly's Service Depot in Piedmont
had convinced him that he was not cut out for time-clock
employment. Al had been one of those grizzled old duffers who
was easy to fool, but still Willy had to waste his days on oil
changes and wheel alignments. This seemed unnecessarily time
consuming when there were so many other old folks living just
off the southern exit ramps of Interstate 95 who could more
quickly improve his circumstances the moment he shoved
his.22 into their mouth. Old women especially scared easily,
and they were usually more than happy to empty their jewelry
boxes for a young man holding a gun. That flattened cat baking
on the asphalt might just as well have been an engraved
invitation to come pay one of them a visit.

The buzz among the Piedmont cowboys was that these old farm houses were deceptive because many of these hovels hid gold mines behind their doors. Every second story man this side of Georgia knew that inside the decaying shacks lived the sort of frumps who placed Uncle Sam's Federal Reserve System in the same category with the greaseball who might slit your throat for a cold beer. To them the bank vault had not been built that was as trustworthy as the tattered mattress upon which they slept.

In helping Willy McCorkle to locate the human fossils who shared this logic, so far Lady Luck had been with him, and he had acquired some decent pocket change. Inside one of these old farm houses he knew some real pay dirt awaited, and Lady Luck would be throwing in her own blow job. Somewhere in an old house like this one those riches were his for the taking.

"Like eatin' corn outa the can," Willy whispered to the empty cab, and pulled the dusty pick-up into reverse. He parked alongside the soft shoulder to inspect the dead animal for any source of identification. It was a chubby calico, and although a mangy creature it did not seem very old. He knew that in places like Loomis Falls where you might wind up porking your own sister it was unlikely any resident would think to place an ID on a dumb cat. The tubby fur-ball he had smeared into the road might not even have been a house cat judging from the look of its coat.

But then again two tons of truck had just passed over it. Cats and old women just seemed to go together, and Willy figured it might be worth a shot to see who was home and to humbly offer the lady of the house some restitution for the pet he had unfortunately killed.

If I might come in for just a moment, m'am, why I'd be much obliged if you'd allow me to pay you for your beloved pet lyin' out there on the road. Thank you kindly, and I am so sorry for what I done, m'am, I truly am. So if you'd be kind enough to just open the door ...

The name on the rusty mail box read Hammond. Excepting his pick-up, Willy saw no other vehicles parked near-by, although there might be one inside the shed behind the house. Whether there was a Mr. Hammond around Willy could not tell. It was Sunday and farmers usually did no work on the Lord's Day.

But Willy McCorkle did. He followed the crooked path through the weeds to the house and stepped onto the rickety front porch. A floor board was missing near the screen door, and the half-rotted door behind it had been left ajar. Judging from what Willy could see through the dirty windows and the torn screen, the grey furniture inside looked like early American garage sale. No one very young lived here, that much was damned sure.

He rang the bell. Nothing. He rang again. Still no answer. This was going to be easier than he thought. He pulled the screen door open. Old people's homes always had that same musty smell. No matter where they lived, you walked into a house that had elderly residents and you were assaulted by that rancid liver-and-onions stench of rotting flesh. It was embedded in the walls and saturated itself into every fiber of fabric. But the smell made Willy smile. It meant that he had come to the right place.

Daylight had a hard time finding its way through the grimy windows and filthy drapes, and most of the parlor was shrouded in dusty shadows. This too was good. Willy quickly headed for the staircase. ... and just as quickly he stopped himself cold.

"Jesus--!"

An old woman sat half hidden silhouetted in the shadows, motionless upon a wooden rocker in the far corner of the room. Wrapped in a colorless shawl, she must have been staring directly at Willy all along. Her shriveled hands rested in her lap upon a thick patchquilt blanket, and the dark rodent eyes that followed him were set deep inside a head that did not move.

The woman's creased gray-crowned face expressed nothing except its age. Only her eyes differentiated her from someone who was dead, but not very much. Standing before her was a complete stranger who had come uninvited into her home, yet the old woman simply sat in her rocker and stared at him as if she were watching a housefly that had somehow got inside her parlor.

Willy had to gulp air just to catch his breath. "Sorry, m'am," he said trying to swallow his gasps as he approached her rocking chair. "I didn't mean to startle you, but I guess you sure have returned the favor. See, I think that I just run over what might be your cat out there on the road, and so I figured---"

Nothing. No reaction at all. If not for her eyes Willy would have sworn a corpse sat in the old rocker. He reached into his jeans jacket and whipped out his revolver, pointing the small pistol directly at her forehead. The woman did not even flinch.

"Look, lady, let's fuck the formalities. I don't want to hurt you, okay? Just show me where you keep the money and I'll be out of here in no time flat, and no one gets hurt. You understand what I'm sayin'?" The woman stared at him yet did not seem to know he was there.

"Hun'reds and hun'reds. Prob'ly over a hun'red thousand of 'em ev'ry goddamned day," she said through pale lips that hardly moved as she spoke. Her voice croaked at Willy from somewhere deep inside her throat.

"What?"

For the first time the woman stirred. Although she had been watching him the entire time, her head finally came into alignment with her eyes. " ... a hun'red thousand of 'em ev'ry day since my Jake passed on, that's how many I'm losin'. Even while ol' Nettie Hammond is just settin' here doin' nothin', doin' nothin' but just settin' here countin' 'em as they go, she's losin' hun'reds of 'em. Maybe thousands of 'em."

Willy smiled and slowly let the .22 drop to his side. He wouldn't be needing it. Ol' Nettie was clearly a few eggs short of a dozen. "Okay, lady, I hear what you're sayin'. You're losin' hun'reds and hun'reds of 'em, yes sir, that's just what's happenin'. So while you're busy countin' up all those figures of whatever the fuck it is you're losin', I'm just goin' to step upstairs for a moment and rob your crinkled old ass blind, if that's okay with you. You just stay down here sittin' in that ol' rocker doin' your figurin' loud enough for me to hear you, and I won't have to come back down to blow your goddamned lunatic brains out through your ears. That's a good ol' girl, Nettie, yes indeed ..."

"Just hun'reds and hun'reds of 'em, and me just settin' here countin' 'em ..." the old woman continued as Willy headed up the stairs. She was still babbling when he reached the top, and this suited him just fine. The crazy bitch would have probably done the same if he had dropped a grenade into her lap.

Although there were two bedrooms, only one of them contained a bed. The other was littered with junk piled clear to the ceiling, and Willy figured there was not much point in rummaging for more than a few seconds through the cheap lamps, broken pieces of furniture, and the countless boxes of dusty magazines.

Ol' Nettie must have been quite fond of medical journals. There were hundreds of them in piles wrapped in tight cord and packed to brimming inside dozens of dirty cardboard cartons. Willy picked up a handful of loose copies from a stack of The Journal of the American Medical Association and blew the dust from them, rifling through articles on health and diseases, human anatomy and surgical procedures, features on the brain and the whole shebang.

"Hun'reds, just hun'reds of 'em ..." he could still hear the woman repeating downstairs.

"Crazy old buzzard," he mumbled.

The woman had kept a regular medical library in the small bedroom, but Willy did not find much of interest in any publication that did not come with a centerfold. Maybe this was exciting stuff for a prune-faced hag who probably had not seen daylight since the Nixon Administration, but otherwise the old magazines were completely worthless.

He tossed the dusty journals to the floor and headed for the main bedroom. There was this unwritten law that every person this side of Georgia over the age of eighty understood, a law with dubious logic that stated one's nest egg became automatically untouchable if someone were sleeping near it. Willy McCorkle intended to dispute that logic.

He swung open the bedroom door and stopped dead where he stood. "Whoa!"

The room reeked with a foul odor that was worse than any other part of the house and Willy had to force himself to enter. He opened a window, hoping the stench would not cause him to woof his breakfast. It stank as if some animal had crawled into the room to die, but first decided to spend some time inside a toaster oven. The room probably had not been aired out in months, and the open window did not help very much. It was the kind of smell that clung to your clothes and forced itself through your nostrils to imprint its fetid memory into every fiber of your consciousness, a stink so powerful that Willy had to shove his head out the window to fill his lungs with fresh air.

Waiting for his breathing to return to normal, he yanked out the drawer of the rickety nightstand alongside the woman's bed. When he flipped it over, two pairs of eyeglasses, a dozen pencils, and a set of yellowed dentures spilled to the floor. No gold mine here.

The old bat had to be hoarding something, he thought. They always did.

A sudden breeze blew open the pages of another medical journal that was on the nightstand. Willy would have completely disregarded the magazine, but the woman had apparently marked off a section, underlining a paragraph with a thick red marker. The article was titled Memory Functions of the Brain and it was written in 1985 by some gray-matter genius named Tolbert whose first and middle names had been reduced to initials.

Human brain cells are finite in number. They gradually deteriorate with advanced age, and as many as one hundred thousand of them a day - cells that can never be replaced - simply disappear, taking with them fragments of memory and intelligence ...

Inside Willy's head a red flare suddenly exploded. Hun'reds and hun'reds, a hun'red thousand of 'em a day, he thought, turning the old woman's ravings over again in his memory. His mouth went dry as the synapses within his brain connected to formulate a thought too grotesque to share with his conscious mind.

That smell! That god-awful foul smell was coming from beneath the old woman's bed! Oh, yes indeed, the woman was hoarding something under there, all right ...!

He tore the sheets and blankets from the mattress, stopping to cover his mouth and nose against the putrescence that assaulted his nostrils in thick waves and kick-boxed with his stomach. Clawing at the stained mattress in several aborted attempts at separating it from the screeching assortment of box springs below, he managed to dislodge the whole assembly of rusted springs and musty coverings, and looked into the black space below the area where the old woman had rested her head.

" Sweet Mother of Christ ... !"

Willy gagged up a taste of his own vomit.

They were in there, all right, clumped together in lumpy piles like stinking clusters of dried sponges, a crazy old woman's hedge against the day when her mind had finally subtracted all those dying cells from her brain and left her with neither the memories nor sanity to soothe her. Some of the gray chunks contained long tail-like stems as if Willy had uncovered a cache of disfigured reptile remains. Others lay in fragmented blood-stained nuggets, like misshapen globs of dark clay that had been molded by an insane child. There were dozens of them.

Maybe even a hundred.

... Hun'reds of 'em.

A lunatic's nest egg of human brains!

Willy suddenly realized how quiet the house had become. The loopy old bitch had stopped counting! Some cloudy signal passed through his own brain and told him maybe he ought to turn around. When he did the old woman was standing directly behind him, hovering over him.

"There's just hun'reds of 'em dyin' inside my head even while I'm just standin' here," the old woman croaked. "And Lord knows, a body's got to save 'em as best a body can!"

For a fleeting moment Willy forced a crooked smile at the woman standing over him. Then he saw what she held in her hands.

With both hands grasping the object tightly, old Nettie Hammond held a baseball bat high over her head. "What the?"

A thought raced through his mind that the crazy old broad could not possibly have the strength to do very much damage, not even with the heavy bat. For Christ's sake, he could knock this old crow over with a goddamned feather, so how could the senile bitch ever manage to ---?

It was the last thought Willy McCorkle had before the woman brought the thick bat down like a mallet and shattered his skull.

***

The young man's truck presented no problem for the old woman. She still remembered how to drive one of those four-on-the-floor jobs, and she wasn't so far gone that she had forgotten the way to Marshall's Swamp. Even a toothless relic like her could still remember how to do that much. Besides, she'd done it so many times before with the others.

But those blasted brain cells were drying up so fast, and sometimes it was hard to remember how to work that damned threshing machine the way Jake had showed her. Luckilly, enough of the little buggers had remained inside her head for her to recollect what she had to do. The thresher was supposed to be only for grain, really, and Jake had warned she couldn't put anything too bulky into that thing, else the machine might choke. So she had to cut up everything she stuck into the thresher's long chute, cut it up real careful into little chunks so that the machine could chew it up real nice for the cats. The cats ... all those poor little cats in the shed ...

She didn't really mind chopping this new one up so much. He wasn't a nice fella like some of the others, talking to her like she was some kind of fool. Still, she had to be careful with the young man's head, 'cause those brain cells were so damned important. She had read about the part of the skull that was easiest to crush and she pretty much knew how to bring her bat down directly at that spot near its base at the neck. Maybe she hadn't done too much damage. Brain cells were getting mighty hard to come by, and she was still losing so many of them. A hundred thousand a day, that article had said. Soon it would be time to set another one of the cats out on the road.

She felt sad that she had to do that, they seemed to trust her so. But folks usually stopped because of the cats. Most folks were so kind about animals and old people, it could almost make you cry.

She felt truly sorry about that too, but sometimes a body's got to do as best a body can. After all, she was just saving up all that gray matter for a rainy day. People would understand that. They always did. People always forgave a lonely old woman, even if she was missing a few brain cells.

Even if she was missing hundreds and hundreds of them ...

The End.

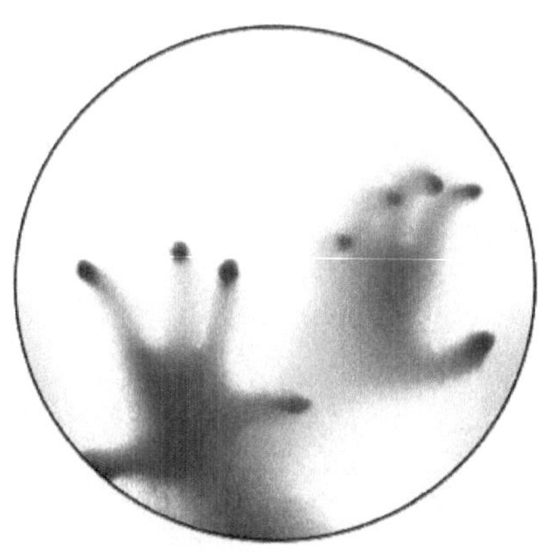

Ken Goldman

Ken Goldman, former Philadelphia teacher of English and Film Studies, is an affiliate member of the Horror Writers Association. He has homes on the Main Line in Pennsylvania and at the Jersey shore depending upon his mood and the track of the sun. His stories have appeared in over 700 independent press publications in the U.S., Canada, the UK, and Australia with over thirty due for publication in 2014. Since 1993 Ken's tales have received seven honorable mentions in The Year's Best Fantasy & Horror. He has written five books: his anthologies of short stories, YOU HAD ME AT ARRGH!! FIVE UNEASY PIECES by Ken Goldman (Sam's Dot Publishers); DONNY DOESN'T LIVE HERE ANYMORE (A/A Productions), and STAR-CROSSED (Vampires 2 Publishers); and a novella, DESIREE, (Damnation Books). His novel, OF A FEATHER, was published in January 2014 by the UK's Horrific Tales Publishers. Ken would be famous except for the fact nobody seems to know who he is. However, he looks forward to the day when he and Stephen King are called to the dais and someone asks "Who is that guy standing next to Ken Goldman?" Please hold your applause until the royalty checks arrive.

Mrs. Tomlinson
Bobby O'Rourke
Physician: Dr. Lotherton
8715-AED19
#90531

"...Unless it is an emergency, you may not leave the room to go to the bathroom. All water bottles and snacks must be off of your desk, and placed on the floor in the front of the room. If anyone would like to use the bathroom or get a drink--or leave the exam and never come back--do so at this time."

None of the students stirred. The empty gymnasium was large but stiflingly hot. No air seemed to circulate. No feet clacked on the burnished golden wood floors, no pencils rapped on any of the ancient desks which were lined up in rows of ten and columns of six. The ropes and rope-ladders that normally hung low to the ground from the ceiling were tied up high in the rafters today. Marty Bloom felt this was sad, somehow. Gym was at least one spot in this dump that was supposed to be fun. The school had managed to suck the life out of this place as well.

His eyes wandered to the red-rimmed baskets and white nets of the impotent basketball hoops that had been folded upward and angled towards the ceiling. The lights from the overhead fluorescents gave Marty a headache, great news for when you're about to take a three-hour test. His eyes found their way to Katie Franco, who sat two seats across and one ahead of him. The lights were playing ugly tricks on her skin, accentuating the colony of pimples on her jaw. Her whole face seemed pasty and malnourished. Marty looked down at his own hand. The skin was a mottle of angry red and unhealthy white. He wondered how his face must look.

Mrs. Tomlinson cleared her throat. Marty's attention came back to the front of the gym. Mrs. Tomlinson was staring directly at him. Marty looked down, but raised his eyebrows as he stared intently at the pockmarked surface of his desk. "If we are all ready," Mrs. Tomlinson said curtly. She continued in her soft, sharp voice: "This section of the exam will take approximately one hour. You may only use a No. 2 pencil, and all your answers must be clearly marked on the multiple-choice Scantron." She surveyed the entirety of the gym, though only six students, scattered amongst the first four rows of the assembled desks, were there to meet her eyes. For the next three hours, this was her kingdom. These students, ones who had dared to miss their scheduled AP World History exam, were her serfs. She owned them. Mrs. Tomlinson was one of the most despised substitute teachers in the school, a disciplinarian routinely called upon by teachers who wished to punish students who disrupted class while they were away. A yellow legal pad and a pen were never far from her grasp, and she was always eager to scribble down the names of kids she could get into trouble in her meticulous, deceptively pretty handwriting. "Well," she said, touching a finger to her wire-framed spectacles, "That was your last chance to escape. You may open your test booklets and begin."

Marty flipped to the first page in his pink test booklet and positioned his Scantron underneath the pencil in his right hand. Rich Reilly, a beefy athlete with football leather for brains sitting in the row behind Marty, dropped his pencil to the floor and snickered. Mrs. Tomlinson whipped around, a shark smelling blood in the water. Even Rich was powerless against that stare, and he got to work immediately.

As Marty filled the first few bubbles in his Scantron, he found his concentration wavering. The political cartoon he was supposed to be analyzing seemed blurred, and he had to read the questions several times before understanding. He brushed a hand through his thick, matted black hair. Certain phrases Mrs. Tomlinson had said kept running through his mind. *...leave the exam and never come back...that was your last chance to escape...* They sounded, well, a little threatening. Not at all like the official guidelines he was accustomed to hearing from the standardized test packs. Marty tried to shrug it off. Maybe Mrs. Tomlinson was just adding a little dash of her bitchy self to the AP stew. It didn't matter.

But the harder Marty tried to concentrate, the harder it became to focus on the page in front of him. His mind felt scattered. Thoughts about how nice a day it was outside, how hungry he was going to be by the end of this stupid exam, how Betsy Delaney's bra had felt last weekend when he got drunk at a party and felt her up on the couch while everyone else was outside smoking. He had fumbled to get over the pliable fabric and pointy wiring of her bra and touch her tits. He only squeezed them for a few seconds before someone had slammed the screen door coming in and startled her. Maybe if he called her this weekend, he could get another shot at those…

Marty realized he had been daydreaming for a long time. He looked at his sheet and saw he had only bubbled in answers one through ten. Then he looked at the clock propped up on Mrs. Tomlinson's desk: it read ten to four. Shit. He had lost twenty minutes, and only had thirty left to answer the remaining fifty questions. His mind had never felt so sluggish. He imagined the break, when he would eat a soggy banana in silence, and then an hour-and-a-half section for two essays, and then the section on short answers. It was a nightmare. All he wanted was to put his head down and rest, just rest.

Then the sound. It was the low, resonant humming of a large string instrument. But this sound wasn't so smooth, had a grumbling, organic quality that made it sound like whatever cello it was coming from had been filled with old chewed-up food. It hovered around him, making a halo around his desk. Marty closed his eyes and concentrated. He could scarcely distinguish that the source of the sound was coming from the front of the room. He opened his eyes. All he saw was the clock and Mrs. Tomlinson, who was engrossed in a paperback, the cover of which featured a busty maiden clinging to the chest of a shirtless pirate.

The sound was coming from her. Her whole body vibrated. Her steel-gray hair, tied up in a tight bun at the back of her head, jangled with the sound. It was like Marty was looking at her through the blades of a rapidly-moving fan.

Marty wondered if any of his fellow test-takers had seen or heard what was happening in front of them. *Was this how a stroke started?* he wondered. He had no idea. When he caught sight of Katie Franco, his eyes grew wider. Katie Franco had fallen asleep at her desk. Her head lay flat on her Scantron, the point of her pencil still erect, ready to fill in the appropriate bubble for question number whatever. Her hair had fallen over the sides of her face, covering her acne. Slowly, Marty turned around in his chair and peered at Rich Reilly. The big senior was unconscious as well, his meaty arms hanging by his sides and his head lolled back so he was staring up at the ceiling. A trickle of drool coated the side of his lips. Marty noticed his eyes were not totally closed, but remained halfway open, as if he were trying his best to stay awake and failing. On Marty's right, there was a clonk as something hit a desk. He looked over and saw an Asian student he didn't know the name of slumped in his chair. The kid's hand had smacked onto the table as his ass had slid to the bottom of the seat. He was two seats away from Marty.

Marty didn't know what to do. What the hell was going on? He could try to reach the Asian kid and poke him in the head with his pencil, but he was too far away. The only other option was getting up out of his seat and going to find someone who could help. But Marty didn't want to do that. He was filled with that regular fear that comes from being the first to do anything. But he was also aware of a deeper fear in his stomach, a childish certainty that if he made a wrong move or an accidental sound, something very very bad would happen to him.

The humming sound coming from Mrs. Tomlinson rose to a loud gurgle. It sounded like she was choking on something and was trying to force it up. It was visceral and violent. A woman like Mrs. Tomlinson should have died from the strain. Her vibrating hands dropped the book, but she continued to shake. A corpse with rigor mortis sitting atop a washing machine.

Something was coming. Marty could sense it, and he did not want to be the only one awake when whatever was coming arrived. Marty, as quietly as he could, laid his pencil down on the desk, folded his arms over his exam booklet, and rested his head sideways on his arms. He shut his eyes, but he could still see through a small crack between his lids. His vision was watery and without definition, but he could see. He was able to make out the shape of Katie Franco, who was still asleep.

The humming-gurgling stopped abruptly. A thick net of silence fell over the gymnasium. Marty tried to control the sound of his breathing, make it regular and sleep-like. A pencil rolled off someone's desk.

Mrs. Tomlinson woke up.

She made another low growling sound as she hoisted herself out of her chair. The legs of the chair creaked under a weight far heavier than what wispy Mrs. Tomlinson should have weighed. A hand dragged along the desk. The sound of sharp nails running along the surface of the desk hurt Marty's ears, but he did not dare cover them.

Heavy footsteps lumbered on Marty's right. Mrs. Tomlinson's breathing sounded phlegmy, the snore of a sick person. She entered the column next to Marty's and walked, as if checking for cheaters. He sensed her go by, a bulk too big to be a retired old crone.

She ran fingernails across the surface of each desk she passed. Marty felt something swish by him long after Mrs. Tomlinson had passed. Whatever it was, it was whipping fast through the air. Marty's mind associated the sound and movement with a-- no, no that was insanity. It couldn't be what he imagined it was.

Then the thing whipped by his ankles, almost touching them. If it had, Marty would have screamed and screamed until he died. Luckily, the thing wrapped itself around a desk leg and then unwound itself. Marty could feel the wind of it as it shot up into the air. A miniscule hissing sound came from the tip of it.

Mrs. Tomlinson's tail batted through the air and under tables.

The more Marty tried to quiet the dreaded idea the more it insisted on filling his reeling mind. Another terrible intuition surfaced: the hissing sound was the tail tasting the air the way a snake tasted the air with its tongue.

Marty felt himself sweating. A bead of it trickled down his back. He was worried it would leave a visible stain. He was terrified the thing could smell him, his fear. Snakes could, couldn't they? He was sure he had read that somewhere once—

The tapping of the fingernails stopped. Marty judged that Mrs. Tomlinson was standing next to Rich Reilly's desk. In the blackness under his eyelids, Marty saw a hulking, heaving presence leaning over the clueless, unconscious Rich Reilly. Marty heard Rich snore, the way he did during all of his classes.

A low-frequency growling sound emanated from Mrs. Tomlinson. It may have been a word, but Marty could not make it out. The tail hissed, rubbed Rich, the sound like someone rubbing two sheets of paper together. Marty's throat closed up. He knew what it was without having to see it. The tail was running up Rich's face, smelling him. Marty tried not to imagine whether the tail was slimy like egg yolks or dry like dead skin, but he failed. Something soft landed on the floor next to Rich: Marty thought it was Rich's baseball cap, the one he wore every day, the one with the disgusting yellow ring of sweat lining the rim. Rich never took it off. It was his lucky cap.

"Reilly," a voice of gravel said. It should have echoed across the gymnasium, but it seemed to die out, fall leaden to the ground. "No hats allowed in the exam room." There was a screeching sound as Mrs. Tomlinson shoved Rich's desk aside so she could stand directly in front of him. Marty almost jumped out of his chair at the sound, the only thing stopping him a survival instinct that compelled his body to remain as still as possible.

There was the sound of heavy hands--or claws--ripping shirt fabric. Mrs. Tomlinson's labored breathing became muffled, as if she had covered her mouth. There were weak thrashing sounds as what Marty imagined to be Rich's feet kicked feebly at the floor. Rich moaned the way you do when something very good or very bad was happening to you. Then a thick slurping sound that lasted thirty seconds but could have been days. Then a sound like paper being crumpled up before being tossed into a wastebasket. Finally, the steady lessening of the sound Rich's feet made against the wood, until they stopped moving.

Marty thought he heard her wipe her lips. Some viscous fluid was flung across the desks.

Mrs. Tomlinson turned and walked down a few rows.

A smell crept into Marty's nostrils. It was not rancid or rotting. It was worse. It was the smell of pool water that had not been cleaned in years (having had an aunt with an above-ground pool, Marty was qualified to judge). The smell was deceptively clean, but beneath it lurked a decay that could only come from years of stagnation and lifelessness. The smell of an old, unaired room mixed with the stinging tang of bleach. Marty fought back the impulse to gag. He tried to swallow as quietly as he could, but he could get no air.

Mrs. Tomlinson was heading back down a row over to his left, coming closer. She ran into the columns of desks, shoving them aside heedlessly.

Marty shut his eyes tighter. His head throbbed. Mrs. Tomlinson was just coming to the side of Katie Franco. Marty watched colorful fireworks go off behind his eyelids even as he listened to Mrs. Tomlinson swing herself around so she was on the opposite side of Katie's desk, facing her.

The gravel-voice: "Ms. Franco," it said. Marty heard the tail slither up from the floor and work its way up Katie's leg. It touched her pimpled thighs and stopped where the cut-off jeans began. "Your outfit is inappropriate for a learning environment," Mrs. Tomlinson said. She shifted her weight and descended on Katie Franco.

Like someone who can't help but peek through their fingers as the slasher movie reaches its climax, Marty opened his eyes. He had half-convinced himself that nothing could be as terrible as all this seemed. He had also half-convinced himself he was, in fact, in the midst of a nightmare, and that perhaps if he confronted the monster within the nightmare he would wake up, sweating but safe in his bed the night before his make-up exam.

He was wrong.

Marty opened his eyes only a crack. He shook uncontrollably. His teeth chattered and the desk rocked under his weight. It crossed his mind as he watched Mrs. Tomlinson do her work that he might bite his tongue off and swallow it. He thought he preferred swallowing his tongue to what was happening in front of him.

Through teary and sweaty-stinging eyes, Marty could make out a gigantic, towering form, the massive upper body dwarfing the lower body. There were two legs, but these legs balanced on gray claws, and they bent the wrong way. The upper body was bulky, hideously muscled, and the color of pond scum. A fleshy shaft attached to Mrs. Tomlinson's back-- the tail--bent and flexed over Katie. It was still smelling her.

Mrs. Tomlinson leaned down onto Katie and kissed her full and hard on the mouth. Katie's face was sucked into Mrs. Tomlinson's mouth, her whole body pitching forward with the force of the suction. Mrs. Tomlinson's hands--grimy, scabbed nubs with sharp protruding appendages--had grabbed the side of Katie's face, pulling her into the kiss. Much of Mrs. Tomlinson's face was indistinct, but Marty could not miss her mouth. It had stretched itself out over the entirety of Katie Franco's face.

Katie bucked in her seat, one hand grasping at the tail which still ran along her arm. Her feet curled up close to her body,

Wicked-Witch-of-the-East style. Her skin turned white and then gray. Her vibrant pimples dimmed and shrank so they made craters in her skin. Her body was collapsing in on itself, concavities forming as when a child sucks the air from a plastic soda bottle. Her skin made a brittle, crinkling sound as it was drawn inward. Everything inside her was being sucked out through her mouth.

Marty could hear a distant whine. Katie was screaming. She was alive, awake and aware for Mrs. Tomlinson.

Mrs. Tomlinson detached herself from Katie and thrust her head into the air, effluence dribbling down her chin. What had been Katie, now a gray pallid human husk, fell back into the chair and wedged itself between the seat and the bottom of the desk. She had shriveled to the size of a suitcase. All that was left of her face was a gaping, liver-colored hole that had once been her mouth. Eyes, nose, ears, all gone. A few white gleams that were teeth clung to the sides of the hole. Thin, fragile clumps of Katie's hair clung to the husk. She was a paper bag.

Mrs. Tomlinson's head turned to face Marty. A huge, syrupy gob of what had been Katy dripped from Mrs. Tomlinson's mouth. Part fluid and part meat, it landed on the floor with a loud plop. The mouth superseded everything--it pushed her eyes and glasses onto her forehead, her nose transformed into two little slits above her lips. Her hair remained in a respectable, matronly bun. The inside of the mouth churned with the innards it had just swallowed, a patchwork of suckers and feelers and cilia that suctioned and shuffled food way down into the gullet. The lips closed in towards each other, making a kissy face.

The tail darted out from behind her. It rushed towards Marty, touching his bare leg and caressing him. Marty pissed himself. A few drops of urine seeping from his pants splashed onto the tail.

Mrs. Tomlinson smiled. "Peeking at another student's test?" she asked. "I'll show you what we do to cheaters."

"No," Marty croaked, surfacing from his horror. "The others…" He knew the Asian kid hadn't been touched yet. And he knew there were two more kids besides him taking the exam, also asleep and ready for harvesting. "Please. Take…"

"Pencils down, Mr. Bloom," she said. She lowered herself so they were eye-to-mouth. He stared into the moving maw as the kissy lips danced to make words in front of him. "Time's up."

The lips fastened over Marty's face.

***

Pictures of six Sieber High School students ran through the local papers for a full year before authorities gave up on finding them. Martin Bloom, Timothy Fong, Katelyn Franco, Josiah Kohl, Richard Reilly, and Alexandra Sierra were never found. Runaways, victims of abduction, no one ever knew. They simply disappeared.

For a time, their disappearance was investigated as a link to another unsolved case, the murder and mutilation of Mrs. Irene Tomlinson, a widowed retiree who substituted at the school. Her body was found in her small apartment two miles from the school when a neighbor complained of a smell like mildew and chlorine coming from her room. Time of death was unknown, but evisceration was easily established as the cause of death. Nothing had been stolen or vandalized, but the destruction of the kitchen sink, which appeared as if something the size of a gorilla had torn its way through to the pipes below, baffled investigators.

Dozens of school official were questioned. None of them could provide any answers, and no one was charged.

Among those questioned was Antonio Delgado, the head custodian of Sieber High school. He said he had stayed late to move the desks after the exam had been completed. By the time he arrived, the students and Mrs. Tomlinson were gone. He cleaned up the gym and went home.

He did not mention that when he went to check if the students were done, he saw that all along the gymnasium floor were scattered what looked like well-worn satchels or bags made from some durable gray fiber. Just more mess, more crap to clean up. "Goddamn kids," Delgado had said. There were six bags in all. He picked up one of the bags and put his fingers at the corners of the openings. He stretched it and let go, the opening forming back into its proper shape. He shook the bag and what he thought were a few pieces of white, hardened gum fell out.

If he had to pick up after these goddamned kids, he figured he'd save the school some money in the process. Instead of turning the discarded bags into the Lost-and-Found, he appropriated them for the school. For many years, the gym teachers used them to store and collect the various balls and equipment used in their classes. Hands of both students and teachers reached into those bags to retrieve something buried way down deep inside.

Only occasionally did a stray tooth fall out.

The End.

Bobby O'Rourke

Bobby O'Rourke is a native of New Jersey, as well as a graduate of both Rutgers University and Union County College. He currently teaches high school and is enrolled in a Master's program. He has had fiction published in The Writing Disorder, and has had poetry published in Spires. Bobby is thrilled to have his work appear in Sanitarium Magazine, and is grateful he is allowed this chance to display his story. When Bobby is not writing, he reads, sings in his car or at karaoke, and performs a little standup comedy. He still checks his closet every night for monsters.

S
The Grinder
Craig Herrick
Physician: Dr. Lichten
6428-SED41
#77808

THE GRINDER ROUSED FROM ITS LONG SLUMBER. The hunger burned inside and could no longer be denied. It had to hunt. The Grinder needed meat.

Now was the feeding time. Instinct led the Grinder as it worked its way to the surface, out into the world once again. To its hunting ground.

Jill Meadows was a jogging fanatic. She obsessed about staying in shape. Though she was forty, she looked a decade younger. To maintain that appearance required dedication and hard work.

She ran in the park every day after work, around sunset. She did at least three miles, often more. She had her iPod set to shuffle and hummed along with the music.

She did not hear the Grinder crashing towards her through the trees.

The Grinder saw the meat running and did not hesitate. The gnawing hunger drove it to feed. It moved quickly through the trees and gained speed as it hit the path.

Jill saw a nightmare burst out of the trees at the side of the jogging path. She only had a moment to see the glowing yellow eyes, the dark scaly hide, the churning legs. And the teeth. So many teeth.

*****

The Grinder barreled into its prey, knocking it to the ground. The beast clamped its teeth onto the meat and tore at it. The flesh and bone parted easily under its powerful jaws.

Jill screamed as the monster chewed off her left leg. She reached down and felt the hot flow of her blood pulsing out of the ragged stump.

She dragged herself backwards as the monster paused to gobble down its morsel. Her leg.

The monster swallowed the large chunk of flesh. Jill watched dazedly as her foot fell out of the side of its mouth to the path, her pink running shoe spattered with blood.

She didn't even have time to scream as the monster leapt at her face.

Sheriff Garth Thatcher barely held down his dinner. His deputy, Jimmy Conley, was not as stoic. He was over to the side of the running path, retching.

The man that had discovered the body was still crying as a paramedic tried to comfort him. Thatcher could not blame him for being hysterical, not with the mess that lay at his feet.

It had been a woman; he could tell that much. Now it was just a hunk of mangled flesh. A leg was missing, the face was gone, and the body cavity had been opened and mostly emptied. The blonde hair was matted with drying blood.

Conley joined him, but would not look at the remains. "Jesus, Garth, what the hell did this?"

"I don't know, Jimmy," the Sheriff responded. "But I don't think a human could have done this."

"Wolves, maybe?"

"Or a bear."

"It has been a dry season. Bears have been known to wander into town looking for food," Conley said.

"That's true. Probably a bear. But this feels, I don't know, savage," Thatcher said.

"What do you mean?"

"Well, I can see a bear running into her, even killing her. It might even eat a part of her, but this seems more like cruelty. Total destruction."

"I don't know, Garth. Did you see any tracks?"

"The running path is hard-packed. Doesn't really hold tracks well.

It's too dark to see anything in the treeline," the Sheriff said.

"So what do you think, then?"

"Gotta be a bear. A big one. What else?" Jimmy shrugged. He had no better explanation.

They followed standard investigation procedures, took all the required pictures, and then let the paramedics bag the remains.

Thatcher said, "Tomorrow we get some of the boys together and hunt us a bear."

He put his hand on Jimmy's shoulder. "Go home. Get some sleep. We're gonna be busy tomorrow."

"I ain't sleeping tonight," Jimmy said. "I'm gonna be seeing that in my head. Probably for a lot of nights to come."

Jimmy was a youngster. He had only been a deputy for two years. He had come home after dropping out of college and Thatcher had hired him because he liked the kid's spirit. That spirit seemed to be gone now.

Thatcher had been the sheriff for fifteen years now. He had seen a lot in his time, car wrecks and the like, but nothing like this. Despite his experience, Thatcher's spirit wasn't doing any better than the kid's.

The Grinder felt more comfortable now. The food had eased the painful hunger. Eased, not erased it. It would need more meat before it could sleep again.

The Grinder left the treeline, searching for more to eat. Its lonely hunt continued.

Thatcher convened a meeting at the station in the morning. Along with Conley, there were three men with hunting rifles.

"Okay boys, we're after a bear today. It's dangerous, so we aren't out to capture it."

"How big?" one of the men asked.

"We're not sure, but pretty big. It killed a woman at the park last night," Thatcher said.

"Mauled her real good," Conley added.

Before they could continue, his dispatcher Peg entered the room.

"There's another one, Garth," she said.

"What?"

"Another torn up body has been found. Old Bob Janks, right on his back lawn," Peg said.

"Shit."

Sheriff Thatcher sent Deputy Conley with the hunters to scour the treeline in the park. He gave them orders to shoot on sight. Then he drove over to the Janks house.

The scene was not any prettier than the last one. Bob Janks had been shredded. At least his face was intact for a positive ID.

Unable to do anything for Janks, Thatcher joined the hunting crew and spent the rest of the day searching. They found no bear or any sign of one. They did find some odd tracks near the site of the first killing.

They appeared to belong to some kind of three-toed animal. None of the hunters could say what might have made them. All agreed it was not a bear.

Thatcher called off the hunt at sundown. He drove home feeling uneasy. He did not think they were dealing with a rogue bear after all. But God help him if he knew what it was.

As Sheriff Thatcher entered the station the next morning, he realized he was dreading more bad news. He stopped at Peg's desk.

"Any more bodies?"

She looked relieved. "No, Garth. Just Mrs. Gillis complaining her dog is missing."

Thatcher released the breath he had not been aware he was holding. "Well, that's good. Jimmy out with the hunters?"

She nodded affirmative and Thatcher went to his office. A memo from the ME notified him they had identified the first victim. Jill Meadows. He would have to contact the next of kin.

"Wonderful," he sighed. Some parts of this job really sucked.

After that difficult phone call, Thatcher decided he needed a break.

"I'm going down to Stan's," he told Peg as he left.

Peg watched him go, feeling sympathy. The sheriff was a tall, lanky man who always stood ramrod straight. Today he slouched like the weight of the world was on his shoulders as he walked away.

Sheriff Thatcher ran his hand through his hair as he walked. It was still dark and thick, but frosted at the temples. He had just had a haircut last week, but needed to sink into something routine to clear his mind.

Stan's barbershop was empty save for Cal Unger and Stan himself. Cal was in his eighties but still active. He liked to pass the day shooting the shit with Stan about sports and politics.

"Morning, Cal," he said.

The old man nodded.

Thatcher sat in the chair and told Stan, "Just a trim if you don't mind."

Stan began his work and the chatter that went with it. Thatcher muttered short answers, not really listening.

"You okay, Garth?" Stan asked.

"Ah, sorry Stan. You heard about these killings?" Stan nodded. "Nasty business."

"I thought it was a bear. I'm not so sure anymore, but I can't imagine what else it could be."

Before Stan could answer, Peg bustled in.

"I'm so sorry, Garth. They found another body."

The Sheriff sighed heavily and started to rise. His eyes landed on Cal Unger. The old man looked dazed.

"Cal? You okay?"

"It's happening again," the old man muttered.

"What? What's happening, Cal?"

The old man's attention focused on Thatcher. "I can't talk about it," he said, rising.

"Talk about what?"

Cal scurried to the door. "Check your archives," he called back and was gone.

Thatcher looked at Stan. "What the hell?" Stan shrugged. "I have no idea."

Thatcher spent the rest of the day at his desk, searching the computer archives. He searched for unexplained deaths, mutilations, murders. Nothing matched his current situation.

"Crazy old bastard," he muttered.

Peg had gone home for the day when Thatcher reached the end of the computerized files. They went back twenty-five years and there was nothing.

He wanted to give up and go home, but it nagged at him. Cal Unger was in his eighties. Whatever he was talking about could have taken place longer than twenty-five years ago, back when Cal had been a young man.

With a sigh, he left his office and went back to the storage room. The older files, all hard copies, were kept here. He knew he would not be able to sleep until he figured this out.

The Grinder feasted. It found a group of targets, two large and two small. They were outside a structure enjoying the cool evening. Just waiting to be taken.

The Grinder was on them before they knew it was there. A large one was taken down first. The other large one tried to put itself between the beast and the small prey. It was no obstacle to the Grinder.

When all the prey had stopped moving, the Grinder settled in to eat.

Thatcher's eyes were red and dry with fatigue when he found it. A dusty file dating back forty-two years. It had not been labeled, so he almost missed it.

The reports in the folder chilled him. That summer forty-two years ago had played out like this one was now. Horribly mutilated bodies scattered around the town and nearby areas. Thirteen deaths over an eight-day period, with no explanation. Then the reports just stopped. There was no resolution.

Thatcher knew the sheriff from back then had died in the line of duty; there was a plaque dedicated to his memory outside the station. But he did not know the details of how that sheriff had died.

The reports did mention that the deputy back then had been Bill Pulliam. Thatcher knew Pulliam. He was long retired, but still lived on the outskirts of town.

Sheriff Thatcher would be paying a visit to Deputy Pulliam in the morning.

Thatcher stopped at the station first to let Peg know where he would be and to grab a cup of coffee. He knew something bad, really bad, had happened as soon as he entered.

Peg's eyes were red from crying and Jimmy Conley looked dazed and pale.

"Oh no. What, Peg?"

She looked up at him and started crying again. "The Hazlets, Garth. The whole family. Even the kids."

Thatcher groped for a chair and sat down hard. "Jesus Christ," he said. "Sweet Jesus." He held his face in his hands.

"What do we do? What's going on?" Jimmy pleaded.

"We're gonna find out. Come on, Jimmy. We need to talk to Bill Pulliam."

They pulled into the driveway and saw Bill Pulliam sitting in a rocker on the porch. He did not look surprised to see them. He just looked tired and very old.

Sheriff Thatcher looked him over as they approached. The top of his head was bald and surrounded by a halo of unkempt white hair. He sagged in the rocker and clasped his hands tightly in front of him. His blue eyes were clear and alert.

"Morning, Bill," Thatcher said.

"I figured you would get to me sooner or later," he said without preamble.

"Why don't you tell us about it, Bill?"

Bill Pulliam sighed. "I had hoped to be dead before this happened again. Then as the years went by, I thought maybe it wouldn't come back."

"Dammit Bill, what?"

"When the killings started, we were just like you are now. Scrambling, frightened, no idea what was happening. We hunted for bears cougars, anything that would make sense.

"Then we found an old-timer, someone like me. Someone that had been around too long."

Thatcher waited impassively, staring at Pulliam. Conley paced the porch nervously.

"It wasn't the first time, you see? It's been hunting this area for as long as people have been here.

"The old-timer called it the Grinder. I don't know what it is, really. Something ancient and evil. Mostly it sleeps, hidden from the world. But sometimes it needs to feed. Then it comes back and hunts."

"You're not making sense, Bill," Thatcher said, but he was cold with instinctive fear.

"It's a monster, Sheriff Thatcher. A thing from a nightmare." Thatcher just stared at him.

"You don't believe me," Pulliam said. "But you will." The silence was as thick as a suffocating blanket.

"I saw it. We tried to stop it. Me, Sheriff Henson, some local boys. We had no idea what we were up against."

"Why didn't you kill it?" Conley asked.

"We couldn't, son. Bullets didn't penetrate its hide. And it's so fast, so fast."

A single tear rolled down the old man's wrinkled cheek.

"I watched it kill three men that night. Sheriff Henson, a couple of the others. The speed, the utter ferocity. It's a killing machine."

"You lived," Thatcher said coldly.

"I'm not ashamed to tell you I ran for my life. We were no match for it. I made it to the car, me and Cal Unger. We got the hell out of there. Tad Thomas escaped too, somehow. It was too much for us."

"What did you do?"

"Nothing. The old-timer had told us it would go away once its hunger was satisfied. We let it finish its hunt."

"You did nothing? Why? Why, dammit? You could have told someone. Called for help," Thatcher shouted.

Pulliam shook his head sadly. "Who would believe us? A flesh-eating monster? No. Me and Cal and Tad swore to never speak of it again. Tad killed himself three years later. He couldn't live with it. Cal and I were weaker. We kept on living."

Jimmy Conley screamed at him. "Bastard. You sorry bastard. Do you know what you did? I saw what it did to those kids. Jesus, the kids."

Jimmy's anger drained away as he broke into sobs.

"You should have told someone, Bill," Thatcher said. "Told me when it started happening again. There's a lot of blood on your hands."

"I know, son. I know." The old man looked away, staring into the distance.

Thatcher led Jimmy to the squad car and drove away. A few minutes later a single gunshot echoed over the Pulliam property, but no one was around to hear it but the crows.

Sheriff Thatcher looked over the men gathered at the station as late afternoon drifted into night. All were men he could trust. Jimmy, Billy Ivey, Ted Buffet and Simon Waters.

All of the men had rifles or shotguns. Jimmy had recovered his poise and was ready to go. The others had listened to what Thatcher had said. They knew it was serious business and were willing to help, but were not sold on the whole monster story.

"We will search along the treeline and go from there. If you see it, call out. Shoot to kill, don't hesitate," the Sheriff told them.

The men agreed and clambered into Ivey's pickup truck. They had decided to take one vehicle so no one could run out on the others. They would all be in this together. They were as prepared as they could be under the circumstances.

They spent the night patrolling, everyone tense and on edge. The darkness seemed to last an eternity. Nothing happened. They never encountered the creature. Thatcher was relieved when morning came to find out there been no killings in the night.

"Maybe it's done," Jimmy said hopefully. "Gone back to hell or wherever it came from."

Thatcher answered, "Maybe. But we're coming out again tonight to make sure. We have to do it right this time, Jimmy."

The sheriff tried to catch some sleep during the day, but it was elusive. He wanted this to be over, for his town to be safe again. For life to be normal again.

That night, he was primed for action despite the lack of sleep. The others looked as ragged as he felt. But none of them backed out of doing what they had agreed to do.

The night dragged on again. Maybe Jimmy was right. Maybe the nightmare was over. The men were spread in a picket line about forty yards apart from each other, searching the wooded area.

Even though Thatcher was prepared, the shotgun blast still startled him. A moment after the shot there was a high-pitched scream.

Thatcher took off in the direction of the noise and the others quickly caught up with him. He made a quick review and saw that Ted Buffet was the man missing.

The men stopped as one when they came upon the scene. Ted was sprawled on the ground, clearly dead. As horrific as that was, it was not what made them stop.

Straddling Ted's chest was the monster. Its head was in Ted's splayed-open body cavity. And it was eating.

"Oh my Lord," Jimmy said weakly.

The Grinder looked up from its kill. More meat stood a few yards away, gaping. It could sense that the meat meant it harm. Instinct took over. The meal would wait.

The monster looked up at them. Its eyes glowed yellow in the night. It had scaly, dark hide and an oblong head that appeared to be nothing but teeth. Ted's blood dripped from those wicked fangs.

It moved. Right at them. Faster than they could imagine. For a moment the men were frozen, shocked into inactivity.

Then Thatcher recovered and fired his shotgun. The other men quickly did likewise. The rounds hit the creature; they could see it stumble with the impacts. It quickly regained its balance and came at them. The bullets did not appear to penetrate the scaly hide.

It came at Thatcher low. Before he could adjust his aim, it leapt. It took him from below, the massive mouth clamping on his groin and lower abdomen, the teeth grinding.

Thatcher felt electric bolts of pain shoot through his body as the teeth rended his flesh. He lost grip of his shotgun as the monster chewed into him and he screamed. Oh, he screamed.

The sheriff's agonized howls broke the other men. They dropped their weapons and ran. Thatcher's screams chased them as they sprinted towards Billy Ivey's truck.

"Oh God, it's coming," Simon Waters yelled.

Jimmy glanced back over his shoulder in time to see the beast bring down Simon. A flash of razor teeth and Simon's leg below the knee disappeared. Blood fountained from the shredded limb as Simon sprawled face first into the ground.

The monster moved up quickly and bit off the top of Simon's head. Jimmy saw a glimpse of exposed brain matter as he dove into the truck.

"Sweet Jesus Billy, go!" he cried.

Billy did. The truck peeled out as Billy Ivey pressed the pedal to the floor. He kept looking in the rear-view to see if it was coming. He never took his foot off the accelerator. Then thing had been so damn fast. Jimmy hugged himself and cried.

The Grinder turned away, unconcerned that some of the prey had escaped. There was still plenty of meat to consume.

The mayor named Jimmy acting sheriff and demanded something be done to make the town safe again. Jimmy uttered platitudes and assurances until the man finally went away and left him to his thoughts.

Jimmy Conley had made his choice. There was no chance that he would go out there again until the Grinder had finished this feeding cycle and gone away again. He told no one about his decision and knew he was damning his soul, but refused to change his mind.

Three days passed, with two more killings. Then it just stopped. After a tense week with no more deaths, Jimmy believed the Grinder must have finally finished its grisly work.

He met with Billy Ivey a few days later. "We can't ever tell anyone what really happened, Billy. You know that, right?"

"Hell, Jimmy, who am I gonna tell? Who would believe me?"

"So it stays between us. Forever."

"I'm not gonna say anything, Jimmy. I just want to stop seeing it in my dreams."

The Grinder burrowed its way into the earth. It was finally satisfied, satiated. Until the hunger came again, it would rest. The Grinder slept and the world moved on.

The End.

Craig Herrick

Craig Herrick was born in New Jersey, but spent his important high school years in Arizona, where he currently lives with his wife Karen, 1 dog and 3 cats. They've been married over 3 years now and spent their honeymoon in the Town Too Tough To Die, Tombstone, Arizona. Craig went to college to study Anthropology with the intention of becoming an archaeologist, but college is hard. Since the bank insists on a mortgage payment each month, he works in the mortgage industry to pay it. In his free time, he goes to baseball games and concerts and writes fantasy, science fiction and horror stories. Though he has several submissions out to various publications, Sanitarium will be the first to showcase his work.

What Doesn't
Kill You

Cindy Little

Physician: Dr. Edgar
9828-SJE41

#19643

PART I

I WOKE WITH AN ITCHY BACK. Your back is the worst place for an itch--especially one this bad. I scooted back and forth across the mattress hoping it could get at what my hands couldn't; after a few minutes of maneuvering it did. Relishing the good scratch, I tossed back the covers, got out of bed and stretched. The wood floor was cool on the soles of my aching feet and the ceiling fan made gooseflesh ripple across my exposed arms and legs. Half awake, I went into the bathroom to get a look at where the beer bottle had hit my forehead. Just a large, purple bump. No blood--this time. Time to get ready for work.

I flinched as I heard my husband Reed rummaging through the refrigerator downstairs. At least I remembered to buy milk the day before on my way home. The last time I let the milk run out I ended up in the emergency room with a ruptured ear drum. Reed didn't work hard, but he hit hard. Why did I stay with him? I asked myself that question every day and every day I had to answer because he and he alone knew what I was capable of. He reminded me daily that *I* was the monster--not him. Some days I believed him. Some days, after feeling the pain and pull of new stitches, I thought that God sent Reed to beat the ugliness out of me. Perhaps one day after I'd done my penance, I would miraculously wake up to a lip that wasn't scarred and a nose that was straight. Or perhaps one day the ugliness would fill me to the brim and over enabling me to rid myself of him once and for all.

Shower first or coffee first? Since Reed was downstairs near the coffee maker and I was already in the bathroom, definitely shower. As the steamy water and coconut scented soap temporarily sluiced away my troubles, I noticed the feathers. Black and tiny and swirling around the shower drain. My comforter must have sprung a leak. Feathers in the bed would

54

also explain the itchy back. As I pushed them down the drain with my big toe, I wished I could stay there all day. The water washed over old scars, temporarily blurring them; hiding them almost enough to make me feel less ashamed of the woman I'd become. I stayed until the water ran cold then stepped out to see the reflection of reality in the bathroom mirror.

"Maya! What the hell is taking you so long? Get your ugly dripping ass into the bedroom and get dressed! I need you to run to the store and get my cigarettes!" roared the dark reflection standing behind me. I jumped and quickly wrapped a towel around myself hoping it would absorb some of the anticipated blows. In the battle of terry cloth and fists I knew the fists would win, but this time the punches never came. Always full of terrible surprises, Reed grabbed a fistful of my hair, yanked off the towel and pushed me onto the bed. "Don't you give me that look!" he hissed as he pushed my pillow down over my face. In the midst of my panicked attempts to breathe, I felt Reed push my flailing legs apart and thrust himself into me. "Hold still or I will shove something into you that will really hurt!" Pin-pricks of light danced in front of my eyes before all went black.

A few minutes later I woke up gasping. The chuf, chuf, chuf of the ceiling fan was the only noise in an otherwise silent house. Reed had left. I tilted my head up and looked down at my now dry but still naked body. No new bruises. Apparently he didn't want me dead--yet. I slowly sat up willing the light-headedness to go away and looked over at the bedside clock--9 am. My first class of the day didn't start until 11 so there was plenty of time to run to the store before heading to the university. In a few short hours I would transform from battered wife into Dr. Maya Mendelson, assistant professor of sociology. Ironic, I know. How could a woman be so smart yet so dumb? But Reed knew--Reed knew too much. After getting dressed I grabbed my good luck bracelet but couldn't get it over a large bump on my wrist. More of Reed's work I assumed; that is until I saw what was pushing out of my skin.

Squinting to get a closer look, I saw something like a small piece of bone sticking out of a neat cut just below the base of my hand. I hesitantly ran my finger over the tip and watched as a pin-prick of blood welled to the surface. Whatever it was, it was razor sharp. "Odd" was the only word that came to mind. Reed must have broken my wrist, yet there was no swelling other than the strange bump or blood at the sight of the wound. Instinctively, I turned my wrist in a quick circle and marveled at the lack of pain. I bent my hand forward and everything still felt fine. I bent my hand back and what happened next was something better left in comic books.

A wicked-looking hooked claw shot out of the base of my wrist. The beer bottle must have hit my head harder than I'd thought. I had to be hallucinating because claws don't shoot out of people's wrists. But still, it seemed so real. I hesitantly reached over with my other hand and traced the smooth curve with my index finger. It was cool to the touch and reminded me of a cat's claw, only much larger and with the ability to bend back and up like a rooster's spur. I looked at my other wrist and noticed an identical bump in the same spot. I also noticed the same small, precise cut wide enough to allow a glimpse of the sharp point just below the surface. I threw this wrist back and the claw shot out. I giggled. *This is it*. I thought. I'd finally gone over the edge.

I was jolted back to reality when I heard the phone ring. Apparently I was still able to receive calls in my new talon-filled fantasy world. I carefully picked up, keeping the business ends of my new "accessories" pointed away from the palms of my hands and wondered who it might be--perhaps aliens from the Andromeda Galaxy who found Maya Version 1.0 inadequate; hence they made a few modifications. "Maya?" No aliens. It was my boss, Dr. Margo Williams. "Sorry to call you at home, but you have a visitor in your office. She refuses to leave and asked if you still had the bracelet. She doesn't speak a lot of English, but made it clear that she needs to see you right away because, and I quote, "the rukh is rising".

Rukh? What the hell is a rukh? "Um, no problem, tell her I'll be in soon." Was all I could get out--and even that with monumental effort. Margo apologized once more and said she'd pass the message on to my strange visitor. I had no idea what the message meant or who was sitting in my office nor did I care. I had more pressing problems to deal with. I took a deep breath and forced myself to focus. First, I had to know for certain if I was hallucinating so I grabbed my cell phone, snapped a quick picture of my wrists and posted it online. I would let strangers determine the fate of my sanity. If they said something about the talons, I'd know they were real.

Looking back at the screen, it showed I already had three comments. I quickly scrolled to the comments section. The first one read "Dude!" The second was a spam link showing me where I could meet pretty Romanian girls, and the third said "Cool!". As I looked away from the screen and down at the talon dragging across the mouse pad, I took another deep breath and tried not to panic. More comments would come in later. In the meantime, I decided to opt for as much normalcy as I could. I figured if I was cracking up why not do it in style in front of my Sociology 101 class? Maybe I could finally get

my students' attention. I went to my closet and changed into a long-sleeved dress and paired it with my most comfortable pair of flats because my feet were still aching. Next, I rummaged around in an old first aid kit and found medical tape to wrap my wrists then realized with fresh horror the two small, precise cuts on the tops of my ankles.

This was all too much to handle. My sanity was fast slipping away which brought on a panic attack. I passed out. When I came to, Reed had an iron grip on my shoulders and was slamming my head against the cold marble tiles. He was screaming something about his cigarettes. I could feel a warm trickle of blood make its way through my hair and down the back of my neck. Then more feathers. I watched them as they caught the drafts made by Reed's manic shaking and peacefully float upwards; up and away from the pain, fear, and guilt. I started to float too. *This is it,* I thought. Reed was bashing my head to a bloody pulp. I would soon be dead; but not before I heard the scream.

At first I thought one of our neighbors came to investigate and got a shriek-inducing glimpse of our marital bliss. But there was no one. All I saw was Reed's murderous expression and more feathers. The scream was coming from me. It was a high-pitched wail that exquisitely expressed the guilt, agony, pain and white-hot rage building in me for the past five years. It started as my own voice, but quickly transformed into something I didn't recognize; something inhuman. The bathroom mirror began to vibrate and pop! pop! pop! One by one, the glass light fixtures above the sink shattered. Reed let go of my shoulders and grabbed his ears. Blood began to seep through his fingers as he too began to scream. And then there were the talons. Two more shot out of my ankles and the ones on my wrists pushed out even further. If I hadn't earned my title of monster at that point, what happened next sealed my fate.

Suddenly my body started vibrating. My eyes sharpened, my muscles contracted and at that moment I no longer saw my howling bleeding husband, but a threat to be eliminated. I shot up, stabbed Reed in the chest with the talons and watched his eyes lock on mine and widen in shock. Then with one deft move I pushed my arms down and split Reed's chest and stomach open. I met no resistance despite the flesh, sinew and bone I was slicing through. It was like cutting into an overripe apple. Streams of blood rushed from the wounds and flowed across the marble tiles as we both stopped screaming and held each other's gaze for a moment more. I saw fear, pain, betrayal and hate looking back at me. There was no love, no compassion, no hint of kindness. My brutal husband's nature was laid bare before me in those few seconds and in those few seconds I realized I'd done the right thing. Reed grabbed his stomach in a futile attempt to hold in his exposed intestines and slumped over onto his side. "You murderous bitch." he rasped. "First the baby and now this."

Blood was everywhere. I panicked. I jumped up, slipped on the slickening tiles and fell hard onto the floor. Reed was rasping his last ragged breaths as his eyes glazed over and his body went limp. I took a deep breath, carefully grabbed the corner of the counter and stood up. The talons were gone. My wrists and ankles were back to normal and I couldn't even feel the bumps. What just happened? Obviously *somehow* gutted my husband, but how? Now that rational thought--or whatever it's called in a crazy person--was returning I grabbed the phone and dialed 911.

"911 what is your emergency?" asked the woman on the other end. "Yes, my husband has been, um, stabbed and is losing a lot of blood.

Come quickly." I hung up the phone before I was asked any more questions, peeled off my blood-soaked clothes and stuffed them in a plastic garbage bag. After washing up in the sink and bandaging the cut on the back of my head, I changed into fresh jeans, a t-shirt and my running shoes. I grabbed the garbage bag, my purse and my lucky bracelet, then headed out the front door hoping I never had to look back.

Needing to catch my breath, I stopped at the coffee shop around the corner and ordered a double espresso. I tried to keep my hands from shaking as I paid for my drink and saw there was still blood under my fingernails. The bored, purple-haired cashier didn't seem to notice as he handed me my drink. I took a seat at the bar near the front window and watched as the ambulance rushed past. *I should go back and turn myself in* I thought. Then I remembered Reed's last words. The baby. Why did his last words have to be about the baby?

I started to cry. After getting an odd look from a college student on his laptop, I wiped my eyes and did my best to focus. My phone rang and I could see it was my boss again so I picked up. "Maya? Margo again. Sorry to keep bothering you, but your visitor is getting very agitated. If you'd rather not meet with her, just say the word and I'll call security. I might do that anyway." In the background I heard an angry voice speaking in a foreign language followed by Margo's scream.

I jumped in my seat knocking my espresso to the floor and watched as my cell phone went clattering down after it. For a brief second the coffee shop went still at the shatter of the cup and all eyes turned on me. "Um, sorry." I mumbled to no one in particular. Now looking annoyed as well as bored, the purple-haired cashier came over and helped me clean up the mess. I whispered a quick thanks and handed him a $10 tip. The money brightened his face considerably.

"Hey lady, I know it's none of my business, but it looks like you've had a rough night. You ok?" I gave him a quick nod and watched as he stood up with the broken pieces of pottery. "Hang on for a second, I'll be right back." He returned with a fresh cup of coffee in a paper cup covered with American flags and past presidents. "I know it's not anywhere near the 4th of July, but the boss wants me to get rid of these cups. Here, this one is on the house." he said as he handed me the coffee. I looked down at my cup and saw Thomas Jefferson staring back at me. I had to trust that Margo was going to be ok on her own, because now I knew what I had to do.

PART II

Small mysterious Jefferson Texas has the reputation for being the most haunted town in the state. To this day, fans of the paranormal flock to the small town to stay at the haunted hotels hoping for a ghostly experience. Growing up I called it home. It had been years--five to be exact-- since I'd seen my dad who'd recently retired from teaching engineering at nearby LeTourneau University. We'd always been close until I married Reed. Like most fathers, he cried at my wedding but more out of worry than joy. He never trusted Reed. He told me as much on the night of my engagement. "I wish I could be happy for your sweetheart, but that guy is trouble. I know you can do better." Those words echoed in my foggy brain the first time I was in the emergency room getting a gash on my forehead sewn up. Ten stitches later I knew I had to distance myself from my father because he was right and I was ashamed. I didn't want him to worry so I stayed in touch by phone always promising to come visit when things weren't so busy. Of course that visit never materialized until now. I started crying after I got into the car and sat down behind the wheel. The itch was back. When I reached around to scratch, I felt something sticking out of my shirt and grabbed it. A small, black feather.

The drive to Jefferson gave me plenty of time to think, yet after several hours of travelling deep into the piney woods I still hadn't come up with a solid plan for--for what? Turning myself in for murder? Voluntarily admitting myself to a psych ward? Both? Neither? If it weren't for the blood still under my fingernails and pounding headache, I'd have thought I'd just had a really vivid, really terrible nightmare. I hoped my father could help me sort all of this out--maybe even find me a good lawyer; or psychiatrist. One thing I did know was that despite leaving a crime scene, my actions, horrific as they were, were in self defense. I knew Reed would have killed me had I not killed him first. I killed my husband. The thought made me shudder as I considered what else I knew I was capable of. I couched my morbid thoughts as I pulled up to the shop in the heart of downtown Jefferson. I saw my dad sitting at one of the tables telling ghost stories to a group of tourists and had to smile at my scientifically minded father's choice to run a "haunted" coffee shop in his golden years. I stepped up to the door, caught his eye and smiled. I was home.

After the tourists left, I was swept up in a giant hug from my bear of a father. Stepping back and holding me at arm's length, his eyes filled with tears despite his best efforts to blink them away. "Oh how I've missed you." Was all he could choke out before walking back to the counter and bringing me out a cup of coffee and a sandwich. As I ate, I told him about Reed, the past five hellish years, the talons, and the final grizzly moments before I walked out the door of our house for good. I didn't tell him about Reed's last words or the baby. That was a conversation for daylight hours; outside the company of ghosts. He said nothing the entire time. When I finally finished, he let out a sigh that carried the weight of the world on it. Once again, I had broken my father's heart. At that moment, I desperately wanted to take everything back; to tell him it was all a terrible, tasteless joke and everything was fine. Instead the truth hung in the air between us like a dark spirit who had been let out of a black bottle. After what seemed an eternal pause, he looked up at me. What he said was more than unexpected, it didn't make sense. "Do you still have the bracelet I gave you?"

"The what?" It took me a minute to figure out what he was talking about until I remembered the bracelet he sent me a few weeks before for my birthday. He said he'd bought it from a woman at the famous Khan Al-Khalili bazaar in downtown Cairo while he was consulting on a luxury hotel project. Other than the fact that it was a gift from my father, the bracelet was nothing special. It was a simple circle made of metal and had Egyptian hieroglyphs carved into it. I wore it often and started calling it lucky because whenever I wore it, Reed left me alone. "Um, yeah, I took it with me when I left." I rummaged around in my purse, took out the bracelet and put it on the table. The glyphs had changed. They were the color of blood.

That night I had the dream. I felt the cold floor beneath my thin nightgown and could see the naked light bulb above me swinging on its wire and doing its best to keep the shadows away; to keep *him* away. I couldn't see him, but I knew he was there just beyond the shelves of cleaning supplies and boxes of Christmas ornaments. My lips were cracked; so thirsty. The kitten was mewling and rubbing against my feet wanting milk, but I had none and *he* knew it. I tried to shush it, but the mewling only got louder. He was coming. I knew because I could see the clouded eyes and smell the rot. I woke up screaming.

"Ghosts get the better of you last night?" asked my father as I nursed a cup of coffee at the breakfast table. I apologized for waking him up in the middle of the night and quickly changed the subject to the bracelet. He again told me the story of the lady in the bazaar who sold it to him, but, after giving me a sheepish look, said he'd been holding back some details because in his mind they were a bunch of nonsense. The lady told him it was very powerful and had the ability to protect the wearer. In order for it to work, she needed to see a picture of me and know what I needed to be protected from. Deciding to play along, my father did as he was asked and showed her a photo of me and Reed at a faculty picnic. He told her the man in the picture was who I needed to be protected from. This made me tense up. My father knew, even without me telling him, that Reed was more than just "wrong" for me, he was dangerous. After studying the picture, the woman blessed the bracelet and said it was bound to me by the powers of the rukh--a great mythical bird. To my father's puzzlement, I excused myself and went to the computer sitting behind the counter. Crazy as it seemed, there was a slim chance the talons could be real.

After a few clicks, I was at the picture I'd posted and noticed I had four more comments. I nearly cried with relief. The first two said,

"No way" and "Those can't be real". The third one said, "Nice work on the talons." The fourth and final commenter wanted me to make him a set. My father came up behind me and looked at the pictures. "So there they are. Wow. I guess I should pay more attention to the jewelry I pick up for you in exotic markets. I think it's time we track down that woman; if that's even possible." I gave my dad a quick smile and picked up the phone to dial Margo.

Margo picked up on the second ring. "Maya! Where are you? I've been worried sick! You just disappeared. What's going on?" I took a moment to reassure her that I was safe and needed to take an emergency leave of absence. Still concerned but kind enough not to pry, she told me to take all the time I needed. I couldn't have asked for a better boss. Next, I asked if she was ok after her encounter with the strange woman in my office. "Oh, I'm ok, just shaken; we all are. She came in and asked to see you, and when I told her I didn't know when you'd be in, she got very upset. She kept going on about a bracelet and that you were in danger. Nothing I said or did was able to calm her down. Next thing I knew, she lifted her hands in the air and started chanting--loudly. Of course, by then half the office was out in the hallway wondering what was going on." Margo paused. "What happened next...what happened next was impossible. I don't get shaken often, but this did it. Maya, she turned into a huge bird and flew out a window! I couldn't believe it--still wouldn't except for the black feathers still floating in the hallway."

The rest of the conversation was extremely strange yet soothing. Things were actually starting to make sense in a low budget sci-fi movie sort of way, but still; I was willing to grasp at the straws I was given. The woman explained to Margo that my bracelet was very old and came from the tomb of an Egyptian queen. It held great power and the glyphs on it spelled out the name of a mythical bird called a rukh that was said to be so large as to snatch elephants off the ground. She also said that if the owner encountered great harm, the bracelet would come to life and turn predator to prey.

Part III

The rhythmic whirring and clicking sounds of the machines in the ICU almost lulled Tom to sleep on his feet. Nearing the end of a double shift, he was looking forward to going home and sleeping the morning away. He walked over to his last patient to check vitals and glance at the IV drip. Everything seemed fine. The patient was resting comfortably and, despite miraculous odds, continued to cling to life. Tom wondered what the man was fighting for; what it was that fueled his need to live.

***

*Turn predator to prey...*Those words continued to echo in my mind after I hung up the phone and explained the conversation to my father. His response was immediate. "Get rid of it. Look what it's done to you already! Get rid of it now!" He was right. Nothing good would come from keeping it. *To turn predator to prey..*despite the danger it posed, I couldn't ignore the fact that the bracelet may have saved my life. Still, I took it along with the bag of blood-soaked clothes out to the back yard and lit a fire in the fire pit. I tossed the gruesome evidence of what I'd done into the fire and watched as the flames devoured it.

That night I had the dream again. The cold felt like a living thing; creeping into my bones and making me shiver. I wanted to stand and warm my hands on the light bulb, but I couldn't because I'd have to leave the kitten laying on the floor; no, not kitten, Ava. I had no milk to give her and she was crying. We'd been locked in the basement for days. Reed was in a black rage and pounding on the door. "Shut her up or I will come down there and shut you both up for good!" *He* was there too; watching and waiting. He wanted Ava, but he couldn't have her. He would never have her. I tightened my grip on my sweet baby, scooted back into a corner near the bottom of the stairs and watched as the black shadows beyond the shelves began to take shape and come for us.

When I woke up my sheets were soaked with sweat and tangled around my legs. The funeral was over a year ago, but the pain still cut like it was yesterday. I missed her so much and wondered if I would ever be a mother again. Part of me longed for it, but another part anchored me to the dream I'd just awoken from; reminding me that good mothers don't do what I did. A sudden ticking at the window pulled me from my thoughts. A huge falcon-like bird was pecking at the windowsill. Initially I thought it was after a bug or lizard, but then it stopped and looked directly at me. *Open the window.* The words were as clear in my mind as if someone in the room had just spoken. The bird began to tap at the sill again.

***

When Tom came in to start his rounds the next day he noticed the bed of his miracle patient was empty. *Poor guy, must not have made it,* he thought. He asked one of the other nurses about it and she said the man was in a regular bed because his condition was improving at an amazing pace. "One tough son of a bitch" said the nurse as she checked another patient's file. She told Tom he should pay the guy a visit because miracle wasn't far off the mark. Apparently the patient was awake and eating on his own despite having major surgery on his stomach and intestines just a few days previous. That, and he kept asking for his wife.

***

I opened the window and watched in shock as the bird flew in. Despite its size, it gracefully glided across the room and landed on a rocking chair sitting in the corner. And unlike the falcons I saw as a child while hiking, this bird was much larger and a pure glossy black. Its eyes...its eyes were...before my mind was able to register *human*, the bird had transformed into a beautiful woman. She waited until I released the breath, I

66

didn't know I'd been holding then smiled and in a thick accent said, "Good morning Maya, we need to talk."

I reached out and grabbed the corner of the dresser to steady myself. First talons, now telepathic bird women? I didn't need to ask who the woman was; I knew. After waiting for me to sit down, she told me the following story: "I am Selket, the guardian of the bracelet you were given. It was created by the Egyptian god Horus as protection for the most worthy wife of the Pharaoh. It was my responsibility to choose the wife and show her how to use it. Eventually, the pharaohs fell, but my duties remained. Over the centuries I have chosen worthy women to keep and use the bracelet until the time of their death. Once they've died, it returns to me. I have chosen you as the next bearer because when I took the photo from your father, I sensed much strength in you. It is an honor that comes with great responsibility as the bracelet gives you the ability to kill; and from the kill, it grows in power. This is where I leave you with a warning. Choose your victims well and make sure they die at your hand; for if they do not, the bracelet loses power and the victim grows in strength. The color of the glyphs"

I held up a shaky hand and stopped her mid-sentence.

"The bracelet is gone. I burned it."

***

Tom's miracle man had fled. According to the other nurses, he was awake and agitated because he couldn't see his wife. Despite reassurances from the staff that they'd been trying to reach her, his irritation continued to grow. Finally, in a fit of rage his tore out his IV line, grabbed the bag holding his clothes and wallet, and ran down the hallway. When one of the security officers tried to stop him, he picked him up by the neck and threw him across the hall. The guard hit his head on a parked gurney and fell to the floor unconscious. Not altering his pace, the man ran through the double doors to the ambulance bay and continued down the street.

***

The bird-woman cocked her head and looked at me like a raven studying a shiny coin. With a bemused smile, she reached into the folds of her beautiful red and gold tunic and pulled out the bracelet. It was a bit charred, but otherwise, seemed unchanged. "Maya, you may be a strong woman, but not strong enough to destroy that which was made by a god." She paused to make sure she had my full attention then continued, " The women before you were seduced by the power of the bracelet. They suddenly had great power; power to destroy their enemies and with each enemy destroyed, gained even greater power. At first, many vowed to never use it. The idea of killing another human seemed extreme to them. But they would eventually succumb; usually out of rage. Woe to their husbands' lovers! The rush of power coursing through them always left them hungry for more. And I know you felt that same rush when you attacked your husband." Again, I stopped her and told her to take the bracelet and leave. Reed was gone and that was all I needed to know. Standing up and laying the bracelet on the dresser, she smiled once more and said, "Are you sure? Look at the color of the glyphs. When they are black, the victim has died. When they are red, the victim still lives."

***

Every cell in Reed's body was buzzing. After escaping the hospital, he ducked into a gas station bathroom to change his clothes. After stripping down, he looked at his naked body in the small scuffed mirror above the sink. The angry purple scars and stitches that ran down his chest and stomach were gone. In their place, was smooth, taught skin covering a lithe, muscular abdomen. He felt more than healthy; he felt completely alive for the first time in his life. Digging into the plastic bag filled with his personal belongings, he grabbed out his clothes and changed; leaving the hospital gown stuffed in the garbage can. Realizing he was famished, he headed into the convenience store and noticed with irritation the line of customers waiting on an incompetent cashier.

***

I decided not to tell my dad about the bird woman. She may have retrieved my bracelet from the fire pit, but I knew she was dead wrong on Reed being alive. She wasn't there, watching blood and intestines pouring out of his body. She didn't see the blank, dying eyes. Red glyphs, black glyphs, it made no difference. I chose to believe that Reed was dead. He had to be. The alternative was unthinkable.

***

After grabbing three hot dogs, a large bag of chips, a box of cookies, and a 32 oz. soda, Reed pushed his way to the front. "Hey!" said a paunchy middle-aged man with glasses at the head of the line. "Wait your turn!" Grumbles were heard as the other customers saw what was happening. Reed didn't respond. In his mind, they were insects buzzing in his ears. He was a god. He not only cheated death, he defeated it. With one swift move, he put the food and soda on the counter then turned and punched the man in the face. The man's nose, followed by his glasses, were crushed into his brain from the impact. He dropped to the floor as the rest of the line looked on in horror at the glasses handles sticking out of the wound; pulsating in time to his final heartbeats. As screams erupted and customers ran, Reed calmly reached past the trembling clerk, bagged his food, and walked out to catch a cab.

I took a shower, got dressed and headed downstairs to the coffee shop where the mingled scents of fresh brewed coffee and blueberry muffins greeted me. There were a few locals eating a quick bite before work and a table of senior citizens having breakfast before heading on a bus tour. My father was sitting at a table in the corner and tinkering with some of his ghost hunting equipment while eating a muffin. He looked up when he heard the familiar creak of the stairs and smiled. I grabbed a mug of coffee and headed over to see what he was fiddling with. "New electromagnetic field meters" was his response. He was thinking about expanding his business to include historic ghost tours. Watching him made me love him even more. With such a kind, peaceful intelligent man for a father, how could I have gone so wrong with Reed? The phone rang, breaking his concentration. He picked up the cordless sitting next to him and immediately I could tell the conversation was more than just a breakfast order. His expression went from concern to ashen as he handed the phone to me. "Maya, it's the hospital. They have been trying to reach you for days. It's about Reed; he's alive."

Reed threw open the front door and took the stairs two at a time. He'd called Maya's boss and was told she was on an emergency leave of absence. That was all the information he needed. He knew she'd head straight to her father because they'd always been close. He hated that fact. The idea that his wife loved another man more than him, even if it was her father, cranked his rage up another notch. As he hurried into the bedroom, he accidentally kicked something and heard it skitter across the floor; Maya's cell phone. He assumed she must have dropped as she left the house and left him for dead. *I'm coming for you Maya, and this time you won't walk away.* He thought as he rummaged through the nightstand drawer, grabbed his car keys and pistol, then headed to the garage.

***

The room began to spin. I took the receiver from my dad and grabbed his hand to steady myself. He held it tight with an expression worry and disbelief. The woman on the phone told me that Reed voluntarily left the hospital early that morning. She went on to explain something about a security guard getting injured, but I couldn't follow the conversation because a knot of panic in my stomach grew to consume my entire being. I felt my father suddenly jump and pull his hand away from mine. His wrist was bleeding. The talons were back.

***

Reed pulled into a small bed and breakfast at the edge of Jefferson just as the owners were locking up for the night. An older couple with deep southern courtesies invited him in and put on a pot of coffee while the woman, Kate, tidied up his room. The husband's name was George and he told Reed that he and Kate grew up in Jefferson, got married and traveled the world while he was in the military. When he retired, he asked Kate where she wanted to go next and, without hesitation, she said she wanted to go home to Jefferson. Reed could care less. He sat staring at George like a cat with a wounded mouse and after about ten minutes was ready to leap across the room and tear the old man's throat out just to shut him up. Noticing his words were falling on strange and deaf ears, George stopped talking and went to check on his wife who had finished up and was already in bed. After showing Reed to his room George turned in as well. Laying quietly next to Kate, he waited until he heard her soft snores before slipping out of bed, grabbing his shotgun and leaning it against the headboard. For the rest of the night he laid awake; feeling as though he'd let a monster into his house.

***

I couldn't sleep. Even though my father alerted the local police and double checked every door and window making sure they were locked, I knew Reed was unstoppable. I tossed and turned until I finally drifted off and into the nightmare. This time Ava was in agony. Her cries were weak and higher pitched than before. My tongue was thick with an overwhelming thirst. My lips were cracked and my milk had dried up. I would sell my soul for a drop of water. I could hear Reed above me screaming and beating on the basement door, but my eyes were on *him*. Black, shadowy robes brushed against the floor and a hood that cloaked his face in darkness. He reached out to Ava, but I held her tight; pushing her face against my breast. I desperately wanted her to stop crying--and finally she did. I wept as I placed my sweet baby in death's arms. It was the only merciful choice I could make--take Ava's life myself, let her continue to suffer and die of dehydration or hand her life over to the monster rushing down the stairs with a baseball bat.

***

Reed awoke early the next morning and went downstairs where Kate was making breakfast. The mingled smells of bacon, eggs and hash browns made his stomach rumble. George was already at the table, a cup of coffee gripped in his hands. It looked like he hadn't slept. Kate jumped when she heard the scrape of the kitchen chair on the floor as Reed pulled it out and sat down. They were terrified of him. He could smell the fear and considered giving them a small demonstration of what was making them uneasy; maybe take the fork sitting beside his plate and ramming it into George's eye. He imagined the satisfying "pop!" and bloody ooze dripping into the coffee cup. Kate dished up his food with a slight tremble. The friendly chit-chat from the night before was gone and was replaced with a tense silence. When Reed had sopped up the last bit of eggs with his toast, he asked two questions: where was the nearest hardware store and what was the quickest way to get to Jensen Stillwater's coffee shop.

***

I woke up crying; crying for Ava, crying for coming here and putting my father at risk, crying over the fact that the talons were back; outwardly reflecting the inward monster. I killed my own child. I should have tried harder to escape. The truth was I was too weak to stand up to Reed and it cost my baby's life. Taking a deep breath, I pulled myself together and washed my face. On a positive note, I realized I could control the weapons at the base of my wrists and ankles by calming down and focusing on pulling them back in. When I went down to the shop, I noticed with relief that my father was chatting with George and Kate, the owners of one of the B&B's in town. I was able to offer a quick wave and head out into the warm, peaceful sunshine for a morning walk.

***

Jensen returned Maya's wave and was glad she was able to slip out for some fresh air. He was very worried about her. She'd been through so much. He didn't tell Maya, but he welcomed the chance to face Reed and end this. With his shotgun loaded and propped behind the counter, he waited for a few customers to head out the door before putting up the "closed" sign, locking the door and pulling down the blinds. He was glad Maya had left and hadn't overheard the conversation with George and Kate who were both pretty shaken up about their recent visitor. Reed was on his way. He hoped they could get things straightened out before Maya got back; meaning Reed leaving town peacefully. Deep down he knew his optimism was unfounded, but he still held on to a thin thread of hope that he could find a way to reason with a psychopath.

Reed pulled up to the coffee shop and noticed Maya's father peering through the closed blinds. He shut off the engine, grabbed the pistol sitting on the passenger's seat and slipped it into his jacket pocket. When he looked up, he jumped at seeing Jensen's face in the passenger side window making a "roll down the window" motion. Reed glanced down at the floor and hoped Jensen couldn't see what was in the bag from the hardware store. Not that it would matter later, but knowing what might be coming to him could make things more difficult. Or not. Reed smiled and shook his head as he remembered what he was capable of. Jensen would prove to be no more trouble than a flea to a dog. Rather than roll down the window to chat, Reed took the pistol back out of his pocket, got out of the car and pointed it at Jensen's head. "Maya, where is she? "

***

The walk did me a world of good. It cleared my head and gave me the courage to face up to what I needed to do; and that was to find Reed and end this nightmare once and for all. Mostly I wanted to keep my father safe. He knew some of what my husband was capable of, but not all. I also knew if he tried to stop Reed from seeing me, he would suffer--terribly. As I turned down the street the coffee shop was on, I froze when I saw the car parked in front of the shop. It was the same one that made me cringe every time I saw it pull into my own driveway.

Taking a deep breath, I quelled my rising fear, threw off my shoes and started to run.

***

Jensen didn't say a word. He calmly stepped away from the car window and went back into the shop. Reed was impressed. The old man didn't even flinch at the sight of the gun. He quickly grabbed the bag from the hardware store then followed Jensen into the shop. His calm was beginning to irritate Reed. *Most people would be pissing themselves at this point,* he thought just as he saw Jensen reach over the counter and quickly pull out a shotgun; but not quick enough. Reed shot Jensen in the side just as he was turning around. He fell to the floor in a heap as his lung began to make a hissing sound. Reed sauntered over and kicked him onto his back. "You got a steel set of balls old man. Now, one more time, where's Maya?"

***

I threw open the door to the shop and ran inside. Silence. No one was there. I saw my father's shotgun laying on the front counter and felt my throat tighten as I looked down and saw the pool of blood on the hard wood floor. Where were they? Had my father shot Reed? Had Reed...I didn't want to think about it. Taking a closer look, I saw a bloody trail leading to the backyard. *Please let it be Reed! Please God! Please not my father!* The agonizing scream coming from the back door gave me my answer.

***

I always knew my husband was capable of terrible things, but the scene in the backyard was out of a nightmare. My father was duct taped into his favorite lawn chair; the one he always took fishing. That alone made the whole scene all the more horrific. Reed was violating all that was good and peaceful not only in my life, but my father's life as well. His shirt was soaked with blood and a pair of bloody hedge clippers was sitting in the grass next to what looked like a thumb and two fingers. Reed had a fist full of my father's hair in one hand a soldering iron in the other. Turning to me, he actually grinned and shoved the red-hot tip of the iron into my father's eye.

We both screamed; my father in agony, I in rage.

My fear of Reed suddenly burned away like fog on a day that promised to be bright and hot. I clenched my fists, flexed my ankles and felt my new razor-sharp weapons shoot into place. This time I was determined to finish the job. Taking advantage of the fact that my scream once again burst Reed's eardrums, I ran across the yard and launched myself at him while he was doubled over. I stabbed my talons into his back with all my strength and felt satisfied as they sunk deep into his muscles and sinew. I raked down the length of his body and shredded his back to ribbons then watched as he crumpled the rest of the way to the ground and lay still. Finally, it was over. I pulled the talons back in and ran over to my father who was hovering on the edge of consciousness. Too late did I see the gas can that hit me hard enough to knock me across the yard.

Reed charged and before I was able to get to my feet, he pounced on me and pinned me to the ground. In an instant his hands were at my throat. Over his shoulder I could see wisps of smoke coming from the fire pit and heard my father offer up a moan of agony. Reed laughed. His sooty fingers and bloody teeth made him look like some sort of wild animal. I reached up and opened the side of his head with one of my talons and watched in shock as the wound healed almost instantly. What the bird woman told me was true. Reed had become more powerful--a lot more powerful. His iron grip on my throat tightened and just before I lost consciousness, Reed shifted to the side so I could see my father still taped to the chair and doused in kerosene. A fire had been lit in the fire pit and the chair was dangerously close.

A few seconds later I awoke to more screaming. Through bleary vision I watched as Reed pushed my father's chair into the fire. His body was instantly engulfed in flames. I shook my head to remove the cobwebs and ran across the yard, talons in, screeching in fury. Reed saw me coming and braced himself for the blow; a blow that never came. I dove across the pit, pushed my father's chair out of the flames, and did my best to douse the fire. My heart wrenched as I looked down at the half-blind, burned husk in front of me. Tears welled up as I carefully pulled him from the chair and watched his one good eye flickered open. "Maya." he rasped. "Quickly. I'm dying. Take my life before I go on my own. It is your only chance." At first I didn't understand what he was talking about, but then I

followed his eye to the bracelet and remembered. But could I kill my father? Interrupting my thoughts, he pleaded, "Please sweetheart. Be brave. He must be stopped." Now sobbing, I kissed his charred forehead, told him I loved him, and slit his throat.

My tears were interrupted by more of Reed's maniacal laughter. "Unbelievable! First, the baby, then me, now your dad! I always knew there was something *off* about you." Reed mused. " I tried, with good reason, to beat it out of you. When the preacher said for better or worse, I don't think he meant a baby killing psychopath with giant bird claws!" Sticky lines of drying blood were trailing out of his ears. Looking into his crazy-mean eyes, I saw pure evil reflected back at me. Yes, I had killed Ava out of fear and weakness, but I killed my father out of mercy. The first would always be an excruciating reminder of the power of fear, but the second; the second offered strength and freedom. The man in front of me however, tortured and killed for pleasure. It was all about motive. And in that moment of realization I was finally set free. My back began to itch.

Suddenly I was thrown to the ground with enough force to push the wind out of me. I felt something stretching against the skin between my shoulder blades and I began to scream as the stretching turned to pain. I could hear the rip of flesh and clothing. Looking up and across the lawn, I could see the shadow of what looked like huge wings across Reed's now pale and silent face. Staggering to my feet I felt the breeze catch under the me and lift me up. As I tried to regain my balance, the wings completely unfolded and carried me up and across the yard. Instinctively, I moved the muscles in my back and felt them respond. Within seconds, I was soaring.

I flew. I could see Reed, now small and insignificant, standing in the middle of the yard and next to the smoking fire pit I could see the charred remains of my father. The sight rekindled my sorrow and my rage. I needed to fulfill my father's dying wish and get rid of the monster below me. But how? He was much stronger now and could heal almost instantly. My thoughts were interrupted as a glint of metal from the lawn chair caught my eye and reminded me of something about Reed I had long forgotten.

I circled around the coffee shop. The breeze flowing over my wings--yes wings! was beyond peaceful. I wished I could stay aloft forever and forget the ugliness below me but I knew I couldn't. When I returned to the yard, too late did I see Reed with the pistol. I watched the gun recoil and searing pain rip through my shoulder.

With each excruciating flap of my right wing, I started losing blood. Still, I wouldn't let him win. I gritted my teeth, shot out my talons and headed towards the ground.

As I landed, Reed shot me again; this time in the stomach. I doubled over in pain and watched him saunter over and put the gun against my head. "I win sweetheart." I closed my eyes and saw my father in his favorite chair fishing on nearby Caddo lake. I would be with him soon and able to leave this nightmare behind. Reed indeed had won. He always won. I was stupid to think otherwise. It was then I heard the click of the pistol's hammer hitting an empty chamber. "Too easy; so predictable! You stand there armed with curved knives shooting out of your wrists and ankles and still roll over to me like a lazy sow." The blow came fast and hard across my face. I fell the rest of the way to the ground spitting blood and teeth. Just like old times.

I pulled myself up onto my elbow and saw my left wing spread out on the grass beside me. It was beautiful; covered with the same glossy black feathers found on Selket. With a shift of my shoulder it folded and boosted me to a sitting position. This time, I saw the boot before it was able to connect. In reflex, my other arm shot up to protect my stomach. Reed screamed as he watched the talon slice through his ankle and remove his foot. I couldn't help but smile. *Heal that!* I thought. He still bled. He still felt pain. And he couldn't grow back body parts. It was all the encouragement I needed.

I staggered to my feet as Reed rolled around in the grass holding his now footless ankle. "You bitch! You cut off my foot!" Blood was pouring out of the wound and making him woozy, but with each beat of his heart I could see the stream was slowing. He was healing rapidly. This was my only chance. I shuffled over to where he was laying and stabbed my wrist talons into his sides. His eyes flew open in agony as he screamed. It was the most satisfying sound I'd heard in years. Feeling woozy myself, I prayed that I'd have the strength to fly while holding his weight. I stabbed my ankle talons into his thighs eliciting another satisfying wail, moved my shoulders and felt pain knife through the right side of my body. The wings shuddered, unfolded and began to lift. Reed grabbed the wound in my stomach and squeezed. I nearly blacked out from the pain, but held on and kept moving. A sudden gust of wind caught my wings and did what I wasn't able to do on my own. Finally, me and my murderous cargo were aloft.

Caddo Lake. I could see the shore just beyond town. Reed's strength was returning with lightning speed so I had to hurry.

Pushing the pain to the back of my mind, I redoubled my efforts and sped towards the lake. I looked down and smiled as I felt Reed's leg muscles flexing against my talons as he tried to free himself. "Go ahead. Good luck recovering from the fall." Reed craned his neck around and saw the roofs of Jefferson below. His face blanched. The look of terror in his eyes gave me the boost I needed to make it the rest of the way to the lake. "Please Maya! Don't drop me! I'm sorry--for everything. If you let me live, you'll never see me again!" Turning his head again he saw the lake below and knew exactly what was going to happen. He started to weep; actually weep. Sick and pathetic. I loathed him more in that moment than in all the years I'd known him. Remembering that he was terrified of water and had never learned to swim, I told him, "Walk out of my life? How about swim out." As he began to thrash in panic, I retracted my talons and watched him plunge into the lake.

My strength was gone and I felt myself starting to fall. I didn't care. Everyone I loved was gone. There was no point to living anymore. I welcomed death knowing I at least rid the world of a monster. Unexpectedly, the wind caught my wings enabling me to glide to the shore where I collapsed. Right before I lost consciousness, I saw a large, black bird descending towards me and knew the bracelet was about to pass to the next wearer. My task was complete. My time was finished.

***

My father's grave marker was modest but dignified; just like the man buried below it. I missed him terribly and wept as I laid fresh flowers on top of the newly turned soil. I thought I was dying when Selket found me laying on the shore, but within a few minutes time I opened my eyes and saw her waiting for me to wake up. She told me that because Reed was dead, my powers had grown stronger and my body could heal itself. She also said that because I'd lost so much, she was willing to take the bracelet and let me rebuild a new, happier, peace-filled life. That, or I could take on the responsibility of the bracelet and use it for doing good. She gave me a week to think about it. The sound of a slap reverberated through the still air and drew my attention to a man roughly shoving his crying wife into the back of a car. My back started to itch as I hurried across the cemetery. My decision had been made.

The End.

Cindy Little

Cindy Little is an aspiring writer who loves reading and writing thrillers and horror stories. Her publishing credits include the novella, Intruder and short story Motherhood. Currently she is looking for representation for her first novel, The Van de Graaff Experiment while working on a second cross-genre novel that combines historical fiction and horror. It is about the disappearance of the Roanoke colonists. Cindy also holds a Ph.D. in educational psychology and has a professional background in educational journal editing and research consulting. She lives in Central Texas with her husband, daughter, a pack of mutts and a prairie dog named Ralphie. When she's not writing she enjoys reading, camping, and volunteering at the local zoo.

TOP 10 UK & US

We take a look at the best selling Kindle titles from the UK and US markets

THE HOPE SPOT

R. Donald James Gauvreau delving into the topic of Zombies

THE DEVIL'S DETECTIVE
SIMON KURT UNSWORTH

REVIEWS

The team at gingernutsofhorror.com open their library to us.

Bestselling Horror US

1 The Silent Girls - *Eric Rickstad*

2 Fat Vampire Big Fat Box Set - *Johnny B. Truant*

3 The Remaining: Allegiance - *D. J. Molles*

4 Polar Bears are Forever - *E A Price*

5 Extinction Horizon - *Nicholas Sansbury Smith*

6 The Walk - *Lee Goldberg*

7 The Vanished - *A Suspense Novel* - Tim Kizer

8 Omega Days (An Omega Days Novel Book 1) - *John L. Campbell*

9 Revival: A Novel - *Stephen King*

10 Pines - *Blake Crouch*

Compiled February 1st - February 28th 2015
Amazon.com Kindle Chart

Bestselling Horror UK

1. The River Is Dark - *Joe Hart*
2. The Silent Girls - *Eric Rickstad*
3. Polar Bears are Forever - *E A Price*
4. EPIC: Fourteen Books of Fantasy - *Terah Edun*
5. The Ward - *S.L. Grey*
6. Fat Vampire Big Fat Box Set - *Johnny B. Truant*
7. Shepherd's Cross - *Mark White*
8. The Forgotten Cottage - *Helen Phifer*
9. World War Z - *Max Brooks*
10. Seed - *Ania Ahlborn*

Compiled February 1st - February 28th 2015
Amazon.co.uk Kindle Chart

6 Questions to Answer
When Designing Zombies
By R. Donald James Gauvreau

For those of you playing along at home and just joining us, in the past two months we've been talking zombies. First we talked about why the zombie genre isn't dead, and may well never be. Then we talked about the symbolism of zombies, what zombies have meant to different writers and how we could use a theme to figure out the details of our zombies.

This month we're finishing out with a list of other questions to ask yourself when you're building your zombie menace. These are generally worldbuilding questions by their nature, and I'm an advocate of doing worldbuilding before you create a plot, but in this case, I think that the two go best hand in hand.

Question #1: What is your genre?

Yeah, yeah, I hear you. "Zombies, duh." But I think that zombies themselves can be more milieu than genre, honestly. You have your romantic comedy zombies, for example, and your survival horror, your post-apocalyptic breakdown-of-society zombies.

World War Z was a zombie movie. Something else that it was, which I don't think most people caught, was a disaster movie. Check out that scene in Israel, where the protagonists are trying to break into a building to escape the horde of zombies that is rushing through the streets like a tidal wave from out of The Day After Tomorrow or 2012 (disclosure: I have only seen one of these, but I'm pretty sure there were tidal waves in both).

Because of how the zombies move and act, sweeping people up in a wave of flesh, they come together like a natural disaster, a lava flow or a hungering tornado that tears apart the landscape.

Question 2: What is the scale of the outbreak?

Most zombie stories, especially today, are global pandemics. Don't do it this way just because everyone is, or you might follow your peers right off a cliff, and no, they're not bungee-jumping, they're being lemmings and now you're dead.

Different kinds of stories can be told with different scales of infection. A town may be under quarantine. An island may be isolated. People on one continent may be safe and sound (or mostly sound, anyways), and your story switches between survivors struggling to stay that way on the infected continent, and characters on the other side of the world who are wondering how they can help or how to keep their side of the pond infection-free.

Question 3: How is the infection spread?

As I mentioned last month zombies don't have to be spread just by biting. You could also have the contagion (virus or otherwise) be in the air. Can it remain viable in the water or is direct contact with infected fluids required, and the contagion doesn't survive for long outside of the body?

Can animals be carriers? Can animals be infected? Don't think that just because the answer is yes to either of those that it applies to all animals, either. Some animals are susceptible to illnesses that others aren't affected by, and some illnesses affect certain species differently than others.

It's even possible that, in one species, the contagion causes peaceful behavior, or at least inspires the infected to choose "fight" only when flight is impossible, no matter how hungry they may be.

Question 4: How intelligent are the zombies?

Most zombies just want to nom your brain. They head straight for people, moaning all the way, and don't care that you just sploshed them with gasoline and are about to drop a match down on their heads.

But it doesn't have to be that way. Maybe they're as smart as chimpanzees. Maybe they can figure out doorknobs, or remember things from before they were infected. Maybe there's no change in intelligence at all, just a new, terrible purpose and desire.

Don't forget that there are different kinds of intelligence, either. The kind of intelligence that would allow zombies to exhibit long-term planning or hunt in packs, communicating with subtle differences of moan that constitute a new language, is not the same kind of intelligence that would turn them into a truck-driving, rifle-wielding army.

Even if they're much better at hunting in groups or at using language, than people are, that doesn't mean that they're smarter than people in every way.

Question 5: How long do the zombies "live"?

If your zombies are fueled and preserved by magic, say, then they might go on indefinitely. If they're still subject to natural laws, however, whether they're altered by a virus or possessed by demons, then you need to look into decay rates across different conditions. When do the muscles degrade, what is it like in this temperature rather than that, or in different humidities, what are the effects of a regular thaw-freeze cycle, &C.

And if your zombies are the living kind, then you have to decide if they eat, how well they eat (if their diet is made up of just the Soylent Green then they may get certain diseases, transmissible and otherwise, than if they have a more balanced diet), and how long it will take them to starve under those circumstances.

Question 6: What do your zombies move like?

In parting, don't be afraid to spin off on crazy things. At worst, you may decide that you need to reign things in a notch when you're done. But— and this is vitally important for you to listen to— don't say an idea is stupid or unworkable when you're in the brainstorming process. Leave that stuff for later.

Do work out the reasonable consequences of your ideas once you've settled on them, though. As a general rule, you should be able to expect readers to accept fantastic axioms, or basic rules, but you shouldn't expect them to accept fantastic consequences of these or any other axioms. Basically, having dragons is okay, but either remember to give them a plausible metabolism for their size, behavior, and so on, or make sure to know why they break the rules.

R. Donald James Gauvreau maintains a blog at www. whitemarbleblock.blogspot.com, where he regularly posts story ideas, free fiction, and other goodies, including a free guide to comparative mythology that was written specifically with worldbuilding in mind.

He is probably not a spider.

by Simon Kurt Unsworth

They say, "he who sups with the Devil should eat with a long spoon." If that is the case then I suspect that Simon Kurt Unsworth not only has a long spoon, but one that is also cast from solid silver. His debut novel The Devils Detective is one of those books, that if you believed in such things, was penned by a writer who had made a deal with the devil.

Thomas Fool is an Information man, one of Hell's special brand of Detectives a man who, up until he is given the call to investigate a brutal death, which sees the victim's soul become totally and utterly destroyed, feels as though he is just going through the motions, more of a yes man than an information man. But there is something about this murder that worms his way into his mind. Fool is determined to solve the crime, no matter who or what he upsets. He doesn't care who takes notice of him, or how much attention he draws to himself and his fellow investigators. And as we all know that may not be the best thing to do in Hell.

The Devil's Detective is a is a richly detailed novel that brims with inventive ideas and clever ambitious writing. Unsworth's version of Hell has been painted with exquisitely detailed strokes. Rather than going with the standard vision of Hell, this personal hell has a more of a feudal feel. It has its own towns and cities, some are grand, some are slum ghettos, hell, some are even red-light districts, where humans and devils walk the same streets. At times while reading the novel it almost felt as though we were walking in the same lands as those from the classic computer game Ultima.

However, it is not just the lands that are painted with great detail. Unsworth has gone to great lengths to ensure the lands of hell feel real, much of this is thanks to his descriptions of the class system of the lands. A system that sees the humans at the bottom of a bureaucratic hellhole. Everyone in Hell has to answer to someone. There is a brilliant scene near the start of the book, where the Devils

to whom Fool reports to, have a system whereby they chose who gets to interrogate the corpse. Unsworth's description of this stupid bureaucracy is worthy of anything ever used in Yes Prime Minister.

It says a great deal about the level of Unsworth's writing when the world building and sense of awe and wonder that can be found in this book far outstrips that found in a novel from a real master of the genre. Hands down The Devil's Detective is a far more satisfying read than Barker's Scarlet Gospels.

This is Thomas Fool's story and as such the main thrust of character development is kept for our intrepid detective. Fool's journey from a somewhat nervous and insecure cipher to a man on a mission is handled with great care and attention, which makes for a very strong lead character. The supplementary characters are not as richly detailed which is a pity, as I would loved to have read more about Elderflower.

The Devil's Detective has the capability to be a real breakout novel, one of those rare breeds of a horror novel that manages to escape from the genre and appeal to much wider audience. The balance between the genre trappings and tropes of both horror and crime is perfectly balanced. While some may see the revelation of the story before our intrepid detective this is nevertheless an accomplished crime story.

AC/DC once said Hell Ain't a Bad Place to Be, and you know what when the writing is this good Hell is a damn fine place to be indeed.

For more reviews check out
Gingernutsofhorror.co.uk

About Kit Power

Kit Power lives in Milton Keynes, England, and insists he's fine with that. His short fiction has been published by Burnt Offering Books and MonkeyKettle Books. A trio of thematically linked novella length tales 'The Loving Husband and the Faithful Wife' (plus short story 'The Debt') and 'Lifeline' are available in two volumes via Amazon now. His debut novel (currently called 'The God Issue', but that will hopefully change) is due out in Autumn 2014.

THE DIREFUL POWERS OF ANCIENT WITCHES
By Fran Jacobs and Clodia Metelli

In the ancient world magic was taken very seriously. We can see evidence for this in the numbers of surviving curse tablets in which curses and spells were inscribed against those who the author wished to punish or control. Magic was practised by both men and women and was a part of everyday belief and practice.

But in Greek and Roman literature we encounter the figure of the witch, an exclusively female magical specialist.

In Greek literature, the witches we meet are attractive women, amorous, passionate and, through their arcane knowledge of herbs and incantations, potentially very dangerous. But in later, Roman literature, we meet a series of fictional witches who, by contrast, are often portrayed as ugly old hags, more like the witches we would associate with Halloween.

Despite the striking differences in these portrayals, the ancient witches had a lot in common. They were lascivious, predatory, jealous and ready to use their magical skills with ruthless determination to get what they want, not caring who they destroyed in the process.

GREEK WITCHES

Circe:

We meet Circe in the Odyssey, one of the oldest surviving works of European literature. The hero Odysseus and his men are sailing back home from Troy when they come to the Island of Aeaea, ruled by Circe, daughter of Helios and Perse, a daughter of Ocean.

Seeing the smoke rising from her house, Odysseus sends a group of his men to investigate. Circe greets them warmly and invites them inside, where she prepares a feast, but she has mingled drugs into the food and drink. Once the men had eaten, Circe strikes them with her wand, transforming them into pigs, though with their minds unchanged. She then drives them into her pig sty and feeds them acorns.

Eurilochus, the only man not to go inside, runs back to Odysseus and reports that the men went into the palace, but failed to return. Arming himself, Odysseus hurries off to rescue his men. On the way, he encounters the god Hermes who warns him that he would have no chance of withstanding Circe's magic without his help. He gives Odysseus a mysterious herb called moly, which he tells him will be proof against Circe's enchantments. When Circe tries, and fails to turn him into a pig, Odysseus must threaten her with his sword, at which point Circe will offer to sleep with him. Once he has secured an oath from her that she will not harm him or steal his manhood, Odysseus can safely take Circe up on her offer and she can then be trusted.

When Odysseus reaches the palace, all happens as Hermes had predicted. Once she realises her magic will not work on him, Circe becomes the perfect hostess and girlfriend. After she has changed his men back to their human form, Odysseus stays with Circe as her lover for a whole year. When he decides to continue his journey, Circe tells him he must first seek advice from the prophet Tiresias in the Underworld and gives him detailed instructions on how to get there. This is the first association of witches with the power to communicate with the dead and it will be echoed throughout Greco-Roman literature.

Medea:

Medea was a princess of Colchis on the Black Sea, the edge of the ancient Greek world. A niece of Circe and granddaughter of Helios, Medea stood between the divine and mortal worlds.

When the hero Jason arrives at Colchis on his quest for the Golden Fleece, so that he can win back his throne, the two goddesses, Hera and Athene, persuade Eros to cause Medea, the young daughter of King Aeetes, to fall in love with Jason so that she will assist him. While Medea is stricken with love for the young stranger in her father's court, King Aeetes is less impressed. Seeing Jason's request as a threat to his rule, Aeetes sets Jason a deadly task he must complete before he can claim the fleece. Jason must yoke two fire-breathing bulls with bronze feet, plough a field and then scatter it with serpent's teeth which will immediately sprout into fierce warriors whom he must battle to the death.

To help him, Medea gives Jason a herb that will make him invincible and invulnerable for a day and he easily overpowers and yokes the fire-breathing oxen, ploughs the field and defeats the warriors who spring up from the earth. That night, fearful that her father has guessed that she was responsible for Jason's unexpected victory, Medea flees the palace and joins the Argonauts at their ships. She then helps them steal the Golden Fleece, by lulling the terrible serpent that guards it to sleep by her magic.

The Argonauts then flee the wrath of King Aeetes, only for a force led by Medea's brother Apsyrtus to catch up with them. Intimidated by this larger force, Jason is initially willing to negotiate the return of Medea if he can keep the Fleece. Medea, however, has her own plan and lures her brother into an ambush, pretending she will help him get back the fleece. When Apsyrtus comes to meet her alone at night, he is murdered by Jason. Medea scatters his parts about the island so that her father will be delayed in sending anyone after them as he retrieves the parts for burial.

Eventually, the Argonauts make it back to Jason's city, but Pelias refuses to give him the throne, so Medea tricks his two daughters into murdering him. She promises the sisters that she can make their father young again, if they chop him up and boil him in a cauldron with magical herbs. To prove this works, she demonstrates on a lamb. But, of course, when it comes to Pelias she leaves out the magical herbs and the king is killed. His son, Acastus, drives Medea and Jason from the city.

The two escape to Corinth, where Jason rejects Medea for a new bride. Medea's vengeance is terrible; she not only slaughters their two sons, but sends his new bride a robe and crown smeared with deadly burning poison that melts the flesh of the poor girl and her father, who tries to help her.

ROMAN WITCHES

In Latin literature, the fictional witches we meet tend to be elderly grotesques, their appearance and exploits depicted with ghoulish relish for dramatic effect. These witches can be found in three main literary sources: Lucan's Civil War features the witch Erictho, Horace employs the figure of Canidia in six poems, and there are several witches in Apuleius' Golden Ass.

With the exception of one witch, Pamphile, in the Golden Ass, who is married, they all appear to be unmarried, old women, who are rather unkempt. Canidia goes barefoot and her wild hair has snakes in it, she also has false teeth, which fall out when she's startled, while Erictho's "face is gaunt and loathsome with decay." (Lucan VI 510)

Gruesome Ingredients

The Latin witches have a penchant for rather vile ingredients to use in their spells.

"They will gather bones and noxious herbs, as soon as the fleeting moon has shown her beauteous face," (Horace Satires VIII) comments the fig-wood statue of Priapus, a Roman fertility god. He is situated in a park that was once a burial ground for the poor and slaves, and remains of those bodies still stick through the ground. This makes it the perfect place for wild animals to feed and for witches to come and get ingredients for their spells. Priapus comments that the witches bother him more than the animals and when Canidia and her friend came to cast a spell, he decides to scare them off by splitting the wood of his backside in a loud fart.

Pamphile, in the Golden Ass, has her own laboratory where she casts her spells. She has plants and remains of ill-omened birds, as well as a collection of corpses' limbs and:

"Noses and fingers were in a heap in one place, and in another, nails from the gibbet to which there still clung flesh from the men hanged there. In yet another place the blood of slaughtered men was kept and also gnawed skulls torn from the fangs of wild beasts." (Apuelius Golden Ass III:17)

In the same novel we meet Thelyphron, who took a job guarding a corpse for the night, which was deemed necessary because:

"Thessaly... contains witches who in different localities bite morsels off dead men's faces and use them as additional materials for their practice of magic." (Apuleius Golden Ass II, 21)

Lucan's Erictho uses a lunar poison mixed with unnatural ingredients, such as the entrails of the lynx, hump of a hyena, marrow of a snake fed deer, to bring a ghost back to his body. And like Canidia, she is happy to search among the bodies of the dead, taking bones from a burning pyre or stealing them from hungry wolves, taking the nails out of crucified victims and:

"...on the corpse: she sinks her hands into the eyes, she gleefully digs out the cold eyeballs and gnaws the putrid nails in withered hand. With her own mouth has she burst the noose and knots of the criminal, mangled bodies as they hung." (Lucan's Civil War VI: 540)

If parts from corpses are not sufficient to attain their magical ends, then the witches have no problem resorting to murder as part of their dark rites.

When Canidia's love potion, meant to bring Varnus back to her, fails, she decides to create a stronger one. With a group of her friends she steals a boy and buries him in a pit up to his chin. Two or three times a day they bring him food, that they keep out of reach, so that he will starve to death and "his parched marrow and dried liver might be a charm for love; when once the pupils of his eyes had wasted away, fixed on the forbidden food." Horace Epodes 5

Although this is fiction, such things were believed to be possible in real life, as can be seen from the epitaph for Incundus, a slave boy to Livia Julia, wife of Drucus, son of the Emperor Tiberius: "I was seized and put in the ground. A magic hand stole me away."(CIL VI.19747) It goes on to warn other parents to be careful that the same doesn't happen to their child.

Supernatural Powers

The witches of Latin literature are credited with a number of supernatural powers including shape-shifting into animals and controlling the dead and spirits of the Underworld.

In the Golden Ass, Thelyphron is warned that witches can transform themselves into dogs or flies. And later a witch transforms herself into a weasel so that she can access the corpse that Thelyphron is guarding, and cast a sleep spell over him. She then summons the corpse, also named Thelyphron, to come to a hole in the locked door, so that she can harvest his body parts. Unfortunately, it is the sleeping Thelyphron who responds and has his nose and ears removed and replaced with wax copies, which later fall off when he touches them.

Like Circe, the Roman witches can also inflict metamorphoses on others. In the Golden Ass, we hear of Meroe who transforms an ex-lover into a beaver, because beavers will bite off their own genitals when chased by hunters. She also turns a rival innkeeper into a frog. Additionally, Meroe seals up the womb of a pregnant wife of one of her lovers, who had spoken ill of her. The woman ended up carrying an eight-year-old child around inside her. And when the townsfolk threatened to punish her, Meroe invoked the spirits of the dead to seal them up inside their houses until they agreed not to.

When another lover, Socrates, whom she had kept imprisoned and wretched in sexual slavery, dares to try and leave her, Meroe has no problem taking her revenge.

Aristomenes, an old friend, had found Socrates on the street, dressed in rags, and had taken him to his inn, fed him and cleaned him up. There Socrates told him his story, that after being robbed on the road, he was taken in by an innkeeper, Meroe. She lured him to her bed and afterwards Socrates found himself enslaved to her.

Aristomenes promises to help Socrates flee in the morning.

But, in the middle of the night, the bedroom door flies open, torn from its hinges and Aristomenes' bed is turned upside down, as Meroe and her sister Panthia enter. Meroe stabs the still-sleeping Socrates in the neck, catching his blood in a leather bottle, before reaching into the wound and pulling out his heart. Panthia inserts a sponge to the wound, speaks an incantation, and then she and Meroe lift the bed from Aristomenes, piss on him, and leave. As they go, the door fixes itself, as do the broken hinges.

Aristomenes, afraid that he will be blamed for his friend's murder, decides to kill himself, but the rope of his noose breaks and he falls on Socrates who wakes! The two then set off on the road and Aristomenes convinces himself he had dreamed the whole thing, even though Socrates also reports a dream where someone cut his throat and his heart had been torn out.

Recalling the dream makes Socrates feel ill and weak, so they stop to eat, but as Socrates eats he grows paler and paler. Complaining of a terrible thirst, Socrates goes to drink from a nearby stream and the sponge falls out of his throat and he falls over, dead.

The Latin witches don't just have control over the natural world, but over the Underworld as well. In the third witchy tale in the Golden Ass, we hear of a witch who summons a ghost to murder a man who left his unfaithful wife, after the witch's love potion failed to win him back. And Eritcho, of Lucan's Civil War, is also able to summon the dead, and force them to return to their bodies so that they can speak prophecies. She is so powerful that she can make the frozen blood grow hot and move through the veins and limbs again, she can make the lungs breathe again, and bring a form of life back to the corpse.

"Uncovered are his eyes with gaping stare: there was in him the look of someone not yet living, already dying; the pallor and the stiffness both remain." (Lucan's Civil War VI 750-760)

CONCLUSION

Ancient Greece and Rome were very much male-dominated societies. While men ruled cities, went to war and conducted larger scale business, women had their own spheres of control. Women were responsible for preparing food and drink for the household, making simple herbal remedies for ailments and for cosmetics, and helping each other in childbirth. This meant that women, despite their lack of overt power, had a whole domain of arcane knowledge that men were largely excluded from. If a man became sick after he had quarrelled with or mistreated his wife, could he be sure she hadn't tampered with his food or drink? What did women whisper about together in the women's quarters or the birthing chamber?

While the portrayals of witches in Greek and Latin literature vary greatly between lovesick girls and grotesque old hags, they carry the same message; women crossed in love may have dangerous, disturbing and unpredictable ways of getting what they want or getting even, and a prudent man, like Odysseus should be on his guard.

Sources:

Apuleius: The Golden Ass
Lucan: Civil War

Horace: The   works   of   Horace:
http://www.authorama.com/works-of-horace-5.html
  Homer: Odyssey Books 10 – 11
  Theocritus: Idyll 2
  Apollonius of Rhodes: Argonautica
  Ogden, D: Night's Black Agents,

BIO

Fran Jacobs is a fantasy and horror writer, author of the fantasy series, Ellenessia's Curse (the Shadow Seer, Seer's Tower) and two short story collections: the Rules of War and Other Stories, a collection of her previously published short stories; and the Child-Eaters' Society and Other Stories, which is a new collection of horror tales inspired by the Greek myths. She has a Masters Degree in Ancient History, a passion for zombies, the 80s, cats and cake. She currently lives in Swansea, South Wales, with her three cats, Megaera, Claudia and new addition, Captain Malcom Kitty Reynolds, adopted at the recent death of her beloved Mr Kitty, where she writes full time, crafts 'unusual' jewellery, drinks too much coffee and works on becoming a crazy cat lady.

You can learn more about her writing on her website: www.franjacobs.com/

And follow her on facebook: https://www.facebook.com/pages/ Fran-Jacobs/20371511691

and see her jewellery at:
https://www.facebook.com/megaerasrealm

Clodia Metelli has spent many years studying the ancient world and has an MA and a PhD to show for it. She is now a writer of historical fiction set in ancient Rome, often with a gay romantic theme. Clodia now lives by the sea with her boyfriend and a small black cat called Achilles.

https://clodiametelli.wordpress.com/

From Dark to Light: Matt Shaw and the Ever Changing Horror Genre By Noah C. Patterson

The face of the literary horror genre has been changing significantly over the past ten years. With the popularization of movies such as Saw and Hostile, more and more authors are delving into the realm of extreme horror. And with the rise of small press and self-publication this subgenre is becoming more lucrative, accessible, and popular. This is great news for fans of dark literature and is a dream come true for many authors. Matt Shaw, a horror writer who has been named by one critic as "The Prince of Splatterpunk," has taken full advantage of the growing genre of extreme horror and has found his success in the growing world of self-publication.

Shaw is an author who dabbles in many different flavors of fiction, mostly extreme horror, but also in quiet horror, erotica, and even some normal stories of life's little dramas—but often with some supernatural twist.

Shaw says that he got into writing through an act of sheer boredom. Like most authors today he started writing when he was young—only twelve years old—during a time when his father was laid up. During that period Shaw spent most of his time fetching drinks for his father, playing games with his father, or sitting in front of his mum's old typewriter. That was when he wrote his very first book.

"The book was terrible," says Shaw, "(a parody of Red Dwarf, the old BBC show) but the process was enjoyable." However, Shaw didn't write another novel for ten years. It wasn't until Shaw was seeing a therapist for depression that he started writing again. "I [was] sitting with a psychiatrist discussing a want to die and anger issues," Shaw recounts. "They urged me to write a diary." For Shaw, the diary didn't happen. Instead he wrote a memoir about being an author struggling with depression. "Writing that [memoir] gave me a great sense of achievement and reignited my passion for writing." Shaw had been mostly writing screenplays up until that point.

That was when he decided to start converting his screenplays into fiction. Having dealt with serious depression Shaw began to express those anxiety, fears, and inner horrors through his writing. "It's a good way of cleansing the soul and I recommend it to all people with bad thoughts running through their head."

Shaw quickly realized his talent for writing extreme horror and recognized the ever growing lucrative market for extreme fiction as a whole. Horror has always been a popular genre whether it be supernatural, psychological, or extreme. Shaw dabbles in all forms of horror, a pattern that follows his ever changing moods and tastes. He therefore appeals to many different tastes in reader—thus adding to his own success as a writer of fiction. His many different variations of writing are also his reason for branding his books into three different categories. Black Cover Books, Red Cover Books, and lastly, books with normal covers.

The Black Cover books are for the lovers of extreme horror. These books are disgusting, shocking and generally messy. The Red Cover books are for people who prefer no horror but full on erotica instead. Then the rest of the books are stories which are more tailored to the 'mass-market'. These are the books which don't normally offend readers, they just take them on a fun filled story and help them escape their own lives for a few hours. (Shaw)

Shaw becomes more accessible and readable because of his branding style. It is easy to immediately recognize one of Shaw's books on the shelf or on amazon because of the way he designs his covers. "It is hard for readers to choose books these days," says Shaw. "There are so many to choose from. I figured by breaking my own work into different brands it would be easier for them to choose between them."

However, even among all of Shaw's various styles and genres his most popular books are his Black Cover series. The simplistic cover design was created to "slap people in the face . . . The titles are shocking and scream for them to be read, or glanced at, and there is a massive market for horror such as this."

Shaw loves writing the Black Cover series, not just for the cathartic effects it has on him as a writer, but also to see how far he can push the ticket. Shaw once asked his community of followers if it was possible to go too far in splatterpunk literature. Ultimately, the answer he received was "no." In response to this Shaw said, "I want to prove people wrong. I want to take things too far from them. I want to make them uncomfortable when reading that particular brand of book." Some authors of splatterpunk would disagree with Shaw's assertion, but Shaw himself isn't afraid to take things too far — and ultimately that is what draws much of his readership.

Shaw states that "it's easy to write gore. But if that was all you did write, it would soon get boring for the reader. You can't simply write gore for gore sake. You need a good story to bind it all together. Without that, you lose your audience." Shaw, in his multi-genre writing abilities, understands how to balance character and plot with the stronger elements of splatterpunk fiction. "Any literature is 'good' if it keeps the audience entertained and brings them back wanting more at a later date . . . No one has the right to dictate what is or isn't good literature. It's the readers' choice."

As a self-published author, Shaw has the ability to make these choices about his writing and marketing, choices that may have been limited had he attached himself to any publishing house. Shaw says that the market of self-publishing — specifically Kindle Direct Publishing — changed his life. "I am at the stage where publishers can't offer me anything I can't do myself. I am in complete control of what I am doing and I am saying yes or no to the offers I receive." Shaw is one of many authors who are proof-positive of the lucrative nature of self-publishing.

I know the self-publishing market has a stigma attached to it but I think that's wrong. We can be just as successful as the big boys but we need to work harder for it (trust me, I am on the go constantly with work to keep afloat of things). It's harder for us to find our place in the market, harder for us to get readers, harder for us in general. But then, when you make it, you can sit back and think… I did this. I made this happen. (Shaw)

The self-publishing market allows us to read talented authors who otherwise may have never gotten published. Matt Shaw, a truly dark and twisted mind, has managed to make a significant name for himself among the independent horror community. He has sold himself as a new brand of horror and has been able to support himself through his work. He recognizes that as a writer "the reader is the most important person in your life." Shaw is a horror writer for the masses. His ever changing moods makes him a lucrative source of horror fiction for readers everywhere.

Black and Yellow
Spiders
B.B. Sevilla
Physician: Dr. Peterson
8268-WCT29
#58935

I DON'T REMEMBER THE FIRST TIME IT HAPPENED, but the most recent time it happened before crystalisis it was necrophea.

Necrophea is what I called what I had for almost two years: a certain knowledge both of impending death *and* the irrational wrongness of that knowledge, although that sense of the irrational wrongness is not to say that I knew I would or wouldn't die soon, for naturally none of us can know that. Rather, I was fully aware that the feeling of inevitable and imminent death was based on a psycho-physiological delusion, and not some sort of precognition.

But yet.

But yet I was also simultaneously certain that I was a day away from death.

Although maybe I should word and order that differently. *For two years, I was simultaneously certain that I was but a day away from death, and that that certainty was incorrect.*

It was a strange condition, and while it might exist somewhere in the annals of medicine, I never found record of such a condition, and so I named it myself: Necrophea.

Before necrophea was liquidity, and before liquidity there was eyeblister. Right now, I'm living post-necrophea. Right now, and for the past few months, it's been crystalisis, and I think crystalisis is maybe the most severe of these conditions thus far, although eyeblister was a real motherfucker.

Crystalisis is this, is that one day I saw a line of light whitish-purple crystals growing from the trunk of a live oak in my garden. They were quite small, and I'm sure that with some quick Googling I could identify what combination of fungus and natural calcium was responsible, but what really matters is that upon the very moment I saw them, these light whitish-purple crystals, my necrophea disappeared, and was immediately replaced by a sensation that something was crackling and growing on the surface of my abdomen.

It didn't hurt, what I felt, but it made a lot of crick-crackly noise, and while—just as was the case with necrophea – I knew it was but a delusion, I was simultaneously certain of the existence of the growth; as soon as I stumbled inside and up over to my bathroom mirror, I lifted my shirt and saw that, sure enough, a flesh-specific simulacrum of the bio-chemical micro-forest I'd just seen displayed had been replicated as a sort of light whitish-purple crystalline bacteriophage that started at my navel and moved bilaterally (though asymmetrically) out to about mid-side. I touched the thing, and it crackled and spread to my finger, but once on my finger it burrowed down into the skin of my hand.

In contrast to the disappearing gunk on my finger, the purple crystals at my core remained extant until about an hour later, when the feeling shifted from one of growth to one of movement, and when I lifted my shirt again, I saw the phage had been replaced by what looked like an undulating hive of black and yellow spiders competing for food or position.

During these last few following months the condition has manifested itself differently every day, and on some days it undergoes a series of shifts in form that increase in ferocity as the day goes on. I've stuck with "crystalisis" for the pathology's nomenclature because that was what I originally called it, and furthermore, in many ways I don't really choose what I call these conditions anyway, but, in fact, the forms are only crystalline about, say, 30% of the time. And there really is no correlation between whether or not the condition manifests as crystalline and whether or not it is awful. Or if there is a correlation, I haven't discerned a pattern.

Today, for example, has been comparatively fine, as the center of the condition at my abdomen has been a relatively silent thatch of what looks like a scab made of yellow wicker, but two days ago on Thursday the thing was a real motherfucker, because it started with a pulsing swath of red crystalline, and as the day progressed the red became blue and then white, and upon the bright whitening of the crystals – this would have been at about 1:30 on Thursday afternoon – they jumped from my abdomen to inside my left nostril and crackle-cloggingly to within both ears, and the ones in my ears wouldn't stop moving and wouldn't stop biting me. So.

So some days it's crystalline and relatively benign, and some days it's crystalline and brutal. Some days it starts as a mess of squirming scorpions, and yet, quite counterintuitively, some of those scorpion days are perfectly quiet and manageable.

I think the closest I can come to a hard-and-fast rule is that essentially any day that there is head or neck involvement is a bad day. When I couldn't swallow because my throat was lined with fingernails and hair, I had to call off of work, and when my eyes were glossed over with scales I had to drown my cat in the bathtub.

This is why I'm worried that crystalisis is maybe the worst, because while I know I got up to some terribly sticky business during eyeblister, eyeblister was merely a measurably ferocious evolution which started itchy in the morning and ended with screaming at midnight. Once I knew the pattern, I knew when to keep myself away from people and things: morning, fine/ evening not.

But with crystalisis I simply cannot know.

The End.

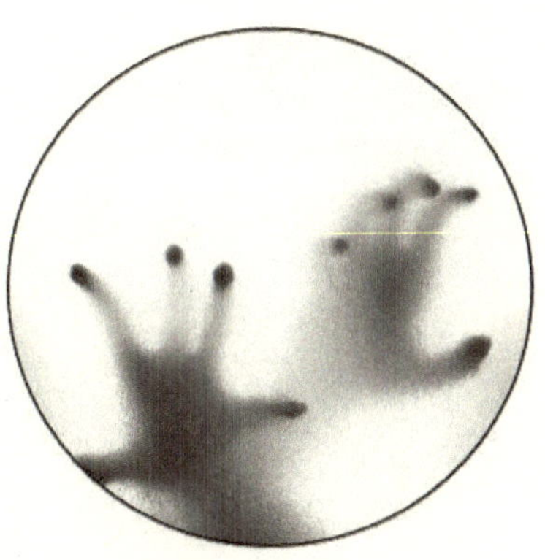

B.B. Sevilla

No Details Released at This Time

The Muse
Jessica Barber
Physician: Dr. Peterson
8268-WCT29
#17216

"SO THIS IS THE PLACE?" I roll down the passenger window for a better look. Crisp air floods the car's warm interior. "Wow, they weren't kidding. It really is an historic house."

Derek pulls into the winding driveway. "I don't get that." "What?" I say.

"Why they say 'an historic' when 'h' isn't a vowel?"

"Google it *after* you help us get our bags inside," my best friend, Alexandra, says from the back seat.

"Fine, fine," Derek says. "Staunch my inquiring mind and use me for my brawn."

Alex snorts. "Yeah, because you're such a He-Man."

Derek is already out of the car, head cocked back, looking up at the 1930s stone sprawler.

Set on a leaf-strewn hill, Cobbler House looms over us. The wind picks up as we exit the car. Skeletal oak and maple branches knock and scratch together. The few leaves still clinging to life—all reds and flaming oranges this late in the Connecticut fall—whisper in the gust like old ladies at a funeral.

"Hi."

I jump and Alex chirps a scream.

"Did you find it okay?" The woman's voice comes from somewhere up the hill. "Welcome to Cobbler House."

I shield my eyes and squint against the mid-afternoon sun. "You must be Nancy."

"That's me." Nancy walks down the meandering flagstone stairway, hand extended.

"I'm Molly." I take her hand. Her heavy rings are cold in my palm. I'm glad to let go. "This is Alexandra. And Derek, my boyfriend. But he's not staying."

"I'm just the chauffeur," he says.

I notice the cars in the driveway. "Who else is here?"

"Two women," Nancy says. "One got here before lunch. The other, about an hour ago. Let's go on in."

Alex and I exchange smiles and skip up the steps.

"I guess I'll bring your things, then." Derek calls.

"I'm so excited to see inside." The flagstone path leads us around the corner to a stone patio.

"Too bad it's so cold," Alex says. "This place must rock in the summer. Look. A hammock. And fire pit. That must be the studio back there." She points to a guest house up the hill at the tree line.

Nancy opens the door to what will be our home for the next three days.

"What a kitchen." Alex says.

Nancy beams. "Completely updated, of course."

The granite and stainless steel gleam. Yet, Nancy's kept much of the original detail. Dark-stained paneling climbs the walls from floor to chair rail with matching beams crisscrossing the high ceiling.

I wrap my wool sweater-coat tight around me against the bite in the air and drop my purse on the kitchen table but immediately pick it up again. "Can I put this here?" The heavily-carved Gothic piece would be better-suited for a European monastery than a New England Kitchen. Sunbeams shoot through a stained glass window, casting colored shapes onto the tabletop. The matching chairs are museum pieces. I expect to see rope blocking them off and those little signs that say: *do not sit.*

Nancy smiles. "Don't worry, the antiques are all usable. All the modern amenities with the charm of the past."

You just *know* she rehearsed that line.

"Gas range. Dishwasher," Nancy ticks off. "Coffee pot."

"Alright." I say. "I'll need *all* the coffee."

"Hi." A white-haired woman wearing a sweater with fruit bowl motif appliques emerges from the hall. The original hardwoods creak under her pristine Keds. "Isn't this place great? I'm Jane. Haze is in the studio, setting up."

Derek stumbles through the door, barely balancing amid his armload. "Haze?"

"Honey." I rush to help him. "You didn't have to bring all our stuff in one trip."

"Yeah," Jane says. "Hazel Rosenberg. Goes by 'Haze.' She's in the studio."

"Oh." I say from the counter where I'm unloading my snacks. "The painter. This is so cool!"

Alex's grin is ridiculous-big. "We're going to have such a fun weekend. What do you do, Jane?"

"I'm here for some peace and quiet so I can finish this darned blanket for my great-niece's baby. She's due in less than a month, and I've barely started." Jane sighs. "You make *one* afghan for *one* new baby, and suddenly you're the family's personal Linens'n'Things."

"What about you ladies?" Nancy asks.

Alex already has her laptop out of her bag. "Writers." "Well, let me finish the tour and get out of your way."

***

"Wait a minute," Haze says a while later after Nancy and Derek have gone. Haze returned from the studio in time to overhear Derek tell me he'll be back in a couple hours. "Where are you going? You just got here."

I sigh. "A memorial service. I tried to get out of it. You have no idea."

Jane settles onto the chaise in the huge great room, a cup of tea and one of my famous pumpkin chocolate chip cookies in hand.

I pull an ottoman closer to my fireside armchair and snuggle under my chenille throw. I've come prepared: netbook, iPod, chargers, huge-ass can of Chock Full O' Nuts, slippers, and my blanket. Alex pulls on her fingerless gloves, which I'm totally jealous of. The ceilings in here are even higher than in the kitchen, but, before she left, Nancy assured us the gas fireplace would have the place toasty in no time.

"I don't get it," Haze says. Her ash-blond hair is streaked with a stark chunk of white at her right temple. Firelight catches her nose ring, which winks and sparkles at us. "You've crammed both a vacay *and* funeral into one weekend?"

I sip from my first cup of coffee. "It's a family friend. An old neighbor, but he moved away when I was little. My mom's known the guy almost her whole life. She made me call him Grandpa John. But we live close enough for me to attend the service and be back here before bedtime."

Alex pulls her long black hair into a bun and opens her laptop. "I was afraid you couldn't come at all, and I'd be alone—" She looks around at the others, afraid she's offended someone I bet. Alex doesn't do well with strangers on her own, even if they *are* all fellow artists.

"And you need your boyfriend to drive you because...?" Haze asks.

I roll my eyes.

"Her mother," Alex says. She's already changed into her writing comfies: flannel pajama bottoms and a thick sweatshirt.

"My mom's convinced I won't be able to drive safely in my bereaved state. She doesn't get it. I really didn't know this guy. All I remember are the creepy Vietnamese ghost stories he used to tell me. He was into folklore. And my mom can't seem to grasp the fact she and I are two distinct people. If she's sad—"

"Then you must be too."

"You're catching on."

"Seriously," Alex says. "It's easier not to argue."

"Right. By the way, Derek put my funeral dress and stuff in the downstairs bedroom. But I don't have to sleep there if anyone else wants that room..."

"Oh no, sweetie." Haze laughs. "It's all yours. Those mannequins are freak-deaky."

"Dress forms," Jane mumbles. She swallows and sips her tea. "Wow. These cookies are good."

Alex mimes a shiver. "Who puts humanoid statues draped in white silky garments in the basement bedroom of a historic—"

"*An* historic," I remind her.

"*An* historic vacation house?"

Haze clicks her tongue ring against her teeth as she considers. "I'll be sure to mention that in my online review."

"You guys are helping me move those things out of there if you expect me to sleep in there."

"Deal." Haze says.

"And maybe Ruthie will *love it* and steal it away from me." Jane gets up for another cookie. "Don't count on it, dear." Jane's excited squeal carries from the kitchen a second later.

Alex, Haze, and I exchange glances, and with matching sighs, extricate ourselves from our fireside seats to meet, Ruthie, the fifth and final guest for our artists' retreat weekend.

Ruthie couldn't be more excited if she mainlined my entire economy-sized can of coffee. I wish she'd stand still for a second. I can't get a good look at her. There's something extremely familiar.

"Oh my Gawwwd!" she says. "Isn't this place gorgeous? Professional grade range appliances. Gas stove!"

I'm waiting for her to kiss the thing.

"Okay, who's who?" Ruthie unwraps a cobalt scarf from around her neck. If my eyes were blue like hers, I'd wear cobalt too.

Our introductions are punctuated by Ruthie's aggressive hugs. Haze sneers like she might punch her, but in the end, she submits like the rest of us. Ruthie never stops talking or moving for thirty minutes straight. She's in and out, lugging bags, boxes, and crates of stuff plus a tripod and what must be thousands of dollars of camera equipment.

"What is all this?" Jane asks.

"Let's see. Dishware for staging my food. But I'm definitely using some of those." Ruthie points to the glass-fronted cabinets and the blue and canary-colored depression glassware inside. She goes on, gesturing at her gear: "Some linens and fabrics for backdrops. Lighting equipment. Recipe notebook. Ingredients."

I finally recognize her. "You're the internet chef! I *love* your recipes." I point to my chest. "MollyMcCooks."

"Oh my God. You write those super recipe reviews. You'd never believe how many people post responses like 'that looks good,' and 'can't wait to try it,' but you're one of my few fans who *does* try them. *Before* posting." She hugs me again, but this time, I don't mind.

Alex goes from gape-mouth to Cheshire Cat grin. "You mean, all that stuff. Recipes and pictures—"

"For my cookbook."

"And we get to eat your food this weekend?" Ruthie nods, and I swear, even Haze looks happy.

Jane rummages in a bag. There's barely a square inch of free counter or tabletop what with Ruthie's stuff and all the food supplies the rest of us brought, but she manages to find a spot for a wine bottle. "Now that we're all here, let's have a toast to our most productive weekend of the year."

Glasses in hand, we eye each other awkwardly until Haze speaks.

"May we all find our Muse." She raises her glass.

"Wait!" Jane says.

I jump so high, I lose an inch of Pinot.

"We need to do this in the great room. By the statue."

"Statue?" Alex and I say at the same time. "Jinx!" I point at her. "Ha. I win."

"Good for you. I bet you get to cross the street all by yourself too." I elbow her as Jane goes on. "The statue on the mantel. 'The Muse.'" Jane manages quotation fingers without dropping her glass of wine. "That's what Nancy called it. Said it's why artists love this house so much. Come see."

We follow, glasses in hand.

"Really?" Alex says. "That ugly thing? Is it a man or woman?"

"I don't know." Haze leans in close. "Clay. Pretty old. Greek styling." She picks it up and turns it over to examine the markings on the bottom. She muscles it back down with a thunk. "Jeez."

"Woman, definitely," Ruthie says.

"No. Look." I point to the very-male genitalia on the nearly naked form.

Haze shrugs. "Well, if Nancy says this is The Muse ..."

She raises her glass again, and this time we clink and cheer: "The Muse."

We soon have music pumping, and we open a bottle of red to go with the white. Despite our clear differences in age and background, we dance, sing, and generally whoop it up, all the while toasting to our artistic endeavors. My almost-finished novel. Alex's new short story. Ruthie's cookbook. Haze's contemporary oil series. Even Jane's afghan.

"Ladies, I hope you don't mind ..." Alex digs in her backpack and pulls out a bowl.

"*Now* it's a party." Haze says.

"Is that ...?"

"Don't worry, Jane. No peer pressure." Alex flicks her Bic and takes a long pull. She passes it to Haze who takes a hit and hands it to Ruthie.

Ruthie shrugs. "It's been a while, but why not?"

I shake my head when it's my turn. "Nuh uh. I've got a memorial to attend in a little while. No way I'm spending any amount of time around my family stoned."

"Tomorrow then," Haze says and smiles as she helps herself to a little more. "Hey. Do we *really* want some inspiration this weekend?" She finds her bag among the pile on a church-pew-turned-bench and pulls out a pallet knife. "How about this?"

She crosses the room and scrapes a couple jags from Nancy's inspiration statue, letting the particles of clay fall into the bowl.

Alex laughs like a loon. "OMG, brilliant. Come on, everyone. We *all* have to take a hit. You too, Jane."

"I'm a little old to start doing drugs."

"It's pot, Jane," Haze says. "Pot's not drugs."

Ruthie is dancing. Well, she's jumping around in time to Florence and the Machine. I guess it's dancing. "You're never too old, girl." Her cheeks are pink and dewy.

"Oh, well. Maybe a little." Jane takes a pull. It gets her hacking, and she puts a hand to her head. "Wow. I'm dizzy. This stuff really works."

"I think that was the coughing fit." Haze takes her own Muse-infused hit.

Once again, I shake my head when it makes the rounds back to me. "Seriously, guys. My mom can smell if I take an extra dose of cough syrup."

"Spoil sport." Alex says and bursts into giggles.

"Derek will be back soon." But they don't hear me. I slip away from the revelry and head to my creepy, dress form-infested bedroom to change for a funeral.

***

After the memorial, Derek drops me off. "Are you sure you don't want me to come in?"

"It's a girls' weekend. No boys allowed. But if they were, you'd be first on my list."

"See you day after tomorrow," he says. After one last kiss, I head up the hill through the moonless night.

I find Ruthie in the kitchen. She's still a ball of energy.

"What are you doing?" I catch the fragrance of sage, onion, bay.

My favorites.

"This is lunch for tomorrow. I'm getting it going now to let the flavors meld overnight."

I practically put my whole face into the steaming pot. "Oh my God. I can't wait to try it."

"No tasting." She wags her spoon in my face. "There's raw chicken in there."

"Noted." The house lays silent except for Ruthie's bubbling pot. "Where is everyone?"

"Haze is out in the studio. June's downstairs. I think Alex is still writing in the great room."

"Then I'll join her for a bit."

She salutes me. "Go get 'em. I'll come chill when I'm done in here." Alex pounds away on her laptop, alternative music station playing over the cable network. "Hey. How was it?"

I reclaim my armchair. "Could've been worse. The food was good. I hung with Derek mostly."

"How was your mom?"

"Dramatic, but I feel bad for her. She's legitimately sad. She tried to talk me into sleeping at their house tonight."

"But your dad's with her, right? It's not like she's alone." I roll my eyes. "How's it going with you?"

Alex gets this goofy grin. "Four thousand words so far."

"It's barely ten-thirty. Let's see if we can get in a few more before bed. Where's Jane?"

"She likes to watch home and garden shows while she knits. I suggested she might be more comfortable in the downstairs sitting room."

"Oh, I see."

"She's got the little gas fireplace going down there. Your room should be nice and warm."

"I guess Ruthie wasn't interested in the dress form room, huh?" "Not one little bit."

I sigh and fire up my laptop. I get lost in my story for almost two hours.

When I finally come up for air, the room is empty. I vaguely recall Alex vacating for bed some time ago. I stretch and yawn, rolling my shoulders to loosen the muscles. The hallway and bedrooms are dark, but the kitchen is lit up like New Years. I pop in there first.

Ruthie's still at the stove. Mumbling to herself.

"You must have cooked enough meals by now to feed us for a week."

She jumps. "Huh?" Purple-gray smudges have taken residence in the grooves beneath her eyes.

"Are you okay?"

"Fine." Her voice is dead in the air. "Just fine." She positions her body square with the stove, but doesn't move her head. Like, at all. It's a nausea-inducing display of flexibility, and I cringe. Maybe she's a dancer or some kind of yoga queen. Eyes still on me, Ruthie stirs with slow, even strokes, as though trying to hypnotize the soup.

"Okey dokey." My voice is unnaturally shrill in my ears. "Well, don't stay up too late." I try to laugh, but it's not a successful sound. The soup bubbles and steams away. It still smells incredible, but my stomach screams a loud and clear *hells no!* I eek behind her to the fridge for a bottle of water then beeline back to the doorway. I don't know why, but I don't want to get too close. "Good night, Ruthie."

"Night." Her eyes follow me out.

Who would have thought a dark hallway would be less oppressive than a bright and shiny kitchen? I take a shaky breath and let metallic *clicks* and *taps* lead me to the parlor.

Jane knits away, staring at the small flat-screen. A re-run of "House Hunters International" is starting with the volume all the way down.

The gas fireplace casts a cozy glow. And a *lot* of heat.

"Holy crap, it's hot down here."

Jane's head jerks my way, but her expression doesn't change. The needles click and tap. Finally, something registers, and she grins. "Hi, Molly! How was your evening, dear?"

"Fine. How's your blanket coming?"

She looks at the afghan growing in her lap as if she's surprised it's there then jerks her head stiffly in my direction again and beams. "It's coming out well!" She sounds like an actor in an Old Navy holiday commercial. Her grin is way creepy.

"Super. It looks great."

"Why, thank you, Molly!"

She looks back toward the TV, but not like she's actually seeing it. "You want me to turn it up so you can hear?" No response. *Click. Click! Tap.*

"Have it your way." I shrug and head down the short hall to the solitary basement bedroom. Jane doesn't so much as glance my way when I wrestle the two dress forms into the parlor. A few minutes later, she gives no sign of noticing when I stomp past on my way to and from the bathroom.

Despite the heat-spewing fireplace, my room is icy. Even with the thick comforter, I can't warm up. Jane's needles click and tap out in the parlor as I shiver in my bed.

***

A stiff face darts from a dark hallway. His features are rigid, eyes stitched shut with Jane's black yarn. His pallor is that of exuberant health, mannequin-like, with rosy cheeks. All his age-won lines and wrinkles are gone.

When he opens his mouth, I expect feathers to fall from his lips, but only words come out.

"I sure am glad you came to see me." "Grandpa John?"

His tone reminds me of Jane when we talked before bed—too bright, too loud. Maybe because I think of her, she suddenly appears—sofa and all—in the darkness behind him. Her needles click and tap.

"I sure am glad, Molly-Dolls."

"But you can't stay at Cobbler house. It's a girls' weekend. No boys allowed."

"Oh, you don't mean that." He clucks his tongue. "You brought me here, after all. If you didn't want me, you should have let me rest in peace."

Click. Tap! Click. Click.

His eyeballs move; they stretch and bunch behind his stitched-shut lids.

"I found myself some spirits too once. They followed me all the way from Vietnam. Couldn't shake loose of them. But you know a secret, Molly-Dolls?"

His grin is huge. I can see all the way down his throat. He leans close and blasts me with his dusty bird-smell. All feathers and claws. I almost *see* one, a claw, deep near his uvula. I don't want to look closer.

"I learned that spirit's name," he says. "You do that, and they have to leave you alone, see. Leave you alone, or, if you're smart." He taps a fingertip alongside his nose and leans in again. His steamy bird-breath tickles my throat like a feather duster. "If you're smart, you can make that spirit do what you want."

"But, I don't want a spirit."

He clucks his tongue again. Jane's needles click and tap in time with his shaking head. "Too bad now, my girl. Because you got one." His eyebrows arch and his face strains.

"You?"

"Nah, I'm only here for a visit. No, my little doll, you've got another spirit. And she's a doozie." He giggles. The muscles of his face tense. His eyebrows arch and jerk.

I realize what he's trying to do.

"No!"

But it's too late. His upper eyelids tear apart, shredded as if by bird claws hidden within the sockets. The remnants of tattered skin dangle from his lower lids. They hang there by Jane's yarn.

I can't breathe. I'm afraid to. Afraid I'll get bird dust in my mouth and lungs. Then the claws will be in my eyes too.

The flaps of skin sway and brush his cheekbones. When I meet his eyes, I find the feathers. Tightly-balled clumps of them, gray and white and brown. Sharp, bone-white shafts protrude here and there from his cavernous eye-sockets.

"You listen to your elders, Molly," Jane says. "Don't worry about the birds. You just listen."

"Molly, learn that pesky spirit's name, you hear." He leans in closer and opens his mouth until it gapes.

He's going to swallow me.

I sit up in bed, in a strange room, with the smell of ancient feathers in my nose and a scream choking the muscles of my throat.

"Holy fuck. What a dream."

Click. Tap. Tap. Tap!

It's a few beats before I remember where I am.

I scramble into my robe and slippers. I'm still freezing. The dusty smell hangs heavy on the cold, damp basement air, and it coats my tongue. I'll need to brush my teeth to get rid of it. Then I catch a whiff of a sharper, more chemical tinge in the air ... burnt wool, melted plastic. Singed hair?

The fireplace. Jane had it cranked way up.

I follow the *clicks* and *taps* to the parlor and there she is, still knitting away before the mute TV. The fireplace looks okay, but the smell is stronger out here. Huge and cloying and choking. I rub my burning eyes.

"Oh my God J—" I can't talk because muscles in my body freeze up all at once.

The smell is coming from her.

My throat burns now too, and my face pulls into a sneer. I can't control my hands; they pluck at my robe, pulling and twisting the fabric. I finally get my mouth to move, but, at first, my lips stick to the air-dried surface of my teeth.

"Juh-juh-Jane?"

Click. Click. Tap! Click.

Smoke spirals up from somewhere around her midsection, or where her midsection must be. Except I can't see it. I can't see any of her. Aside from the area from her elbows down, only her nose and one eye is visible. She's woven herself a cocoon crafted from yarn, thread, sinewy scorched electrical cords, and *God knows what else* Jane has managed to ensnare in those knitting needles.

She snakes a finger from the cocoon to snag a loose thread from the chenille-covered sofa cushion. Her fingers move furiously. The needles click and tap. As the product of her labor grows, she pauses to vacantly toss it over her shoulder or twine it around her waist. A moment later, she maneuvers with a free ankle to wrap a snaking stretch around her calf.

More billows of smoke join the first.

The wires.

The electrical wires.

How the hell did she? They're not plugged in, are they? That would be impossible.

But clearly it's not.

The first spark breaks my freeze. I bolt across the room and land on my knees at her feet. There's no good place to start but I have to try. I brush no more than a fingertip across a section of coiled mess when a jolt staggers me backward into the wall.

What do I do now?

It's only when I smell Jane start to cook from within her afghan-gone-wrong that I get moving.

Alex's door is open when I mount the steps. A tell-tale bar of light shines between the bathroom door and floor.

"Alex!"

I pound.

She pulls open the door, wiping her mouth with a towel, complexion gone sickly green-gray.

"What's wrong?" I ask.

"Sick. Something I ate maybe. What's up with you?" "Jane. Downstairs. She ... Come see." I tug her hand. "Molly, I need to go back to bed."

I ignore her. Maybe because she feels too crappy to argue, she stumbles along behind me.

We're halfway down when she tugs back for the first time. "What's that smell? I'm gonna hurl again."

"Come *on*."

Tap! Tap. Click!

"Holy shit," Alex whispers.

Smoke fills the room. It hits me then. "This whole house could catch fire if we don't stop her. The power. We need to find the circuit box."

"I've got it!" Alex runs upstairs.

She's already flipping light switches when I reach the main floor. I'm not sure how wise that is given the electrical load Jane's created, but we need light.

Alex riffles through magazines on the great room coffee table and finds a laminate-covered, home-made book. "The house's user manual. I found it when I was trying to figure out how to work the ceiling fan. Let's see ... the studio." I reach the kitchen ahead of Alex.

"Holy shit! It's a sauna in here. Open a window or something, Ruthie."

Ruthie stands right where I left her. In front of that damned stove, hovering over her pot.

Alex slams into my back when I freeze. "What the fuck, Moll?" Alex's shrill voice pierces my eardrum.

My stomach twists and churns.

Ruthie stares at us for a full thirty seconds before she gives any sign she recognizes who we are.

"Molly! Alex! Well, hi there! You wanna taste the soup?"

What's in that pot isn't soup anymore. It's thickened and congealed. My stomach protests the very thought of admitting that stuff into my mouth.

"Ruthie," I say. "This isn't a good time."

The shadows under her eyes have darkened to soot-like smudges. And doesn't move at all. She stands there, mouth slack, arms hanging limply at her sides, spoon dripping dark, herb-dotted liquid to the floor. A fat blob lands on her bare foot. She stands there, like a statue, arm extended. The spoon drips, drips, drips. Like I'm hypnotized, I watch each drop land.

"What's wrong with her eyes?" Alex asks.

I pull my gaze away from Ruthie's feet and really take in her face. "Oh my God ..." The goop on the stove must have distracted me. There's no other way I would have missed it. Her formerly cobalt irises are now faded, almost like they've been bleached.

"Look. She's not blinking. Like, not at all."

It hits me then: she'd been standing over that pot for *hours*. "I think she steamed them."

"You mean, she cooked her eyeballs?"

"Hi, Molly! Alex!" Ruthie chirps like she hadn't already noticed us. "You wanna taste the soup?" As if this idea were a battery powering her body systems, Ruthie becomes animated once more. She raises the spoon and spins. Some of the gravy still pooled in its bowl slops onto the cabinets. She's got that thing in her pot a second later. Then she advances on us, spoon first.

"No thanks. Really, Ruthie. We're not hungry." I shrug away, lips pressed together, and she turns her assault on Alex.

"Not me either. Something's wrong with Jane. We have to"

Ruthie jams her spoon into Alex's mouth. I cringe when it bangs into Alex's front teeth.

Alex chokes, sputters, and coughs. "That was fucking hot."

"How is it?" Ruthie asks. "Does it need anything?" She's at the stove, stirring again, this time with a frantic exuberance that causes the contents to slosh all over the stove top.

"Gee, Ruthie. I don't know. It *does* seem to be missing something." Oh no. Alex is using her pissed off *I'm fucking with you voice*. Never a good sign.

Alex runs her tongue over her upper teeth. "You chipped one." Ruthie frowns, but not because of her spoon-inflicted dental damage. "Let me taste." She slurps back a spoonful and smears a few blobs on her face in the process.

My stomach clenches.

Ruthie smacks her lips. "I know. More of this."

But instead of reaching to her wall of stacked herb jars and sundry seasonings, she rolls up her sleeve.

Alex screams and bends over. The full contents of her stomach land on the restored hardwoods.

What remains of Ruthie's left forearm is a mess of glaring, purple flesh grimed over by crusty dried blood and some still-oozing fresh flow. She grabs a vegetable peeler, slices off a relatively clean bit of skin, and ... *plop!* In the pot it goes. White tendon shifts and flashes near her elbow as she picks up the spoon again. It's then I notice the bloody knives that litter the counter.

"Ruthie!" I say. "Are you crazy? We have to call 911."

Ruthie stirs, a prim expression on her face. She samples the stew or soup or whatever the hell it is. "Still needs something," she says. "I know. One of these." She grabs the huge-ass cleaver and lays her left hand flat on the counter.

"No," I shout. "Alex, quick. Grab her."

But Alex is still puking, and I'm too slow. Ruthie manages to bring the cleaver down on her hand before I get there. Two fingers are cut clean off right below the second knuckle, and a third is almost there. "One should do it," Ruthie says. "But I'll keep these, just in case." She drops the second finger into an empty mason jar. Ignoring the spouts and spurts of blood shooting to cover the counter, she finishes the job on the third.

I stagger away from her. "Come on, Al." I gesture at the door with my eyes.

To get outside, we'll need to scoot behind Ruthie. I pray she doesn't turn the knife on us next. There's no way any of my fingers could make that mess taste any better.

"I swallowed some of it, Moll." She urps and puts a hand to her mouth.

"Let's go."

I inch to my left. Alex snaps out of it a second later and books right by me. Ruthie doesn't even notice.

The cold night air is a dream after the herbed-steam of the kitchen.

I gulp huge lungfuls.

"Let's just get out of here." Alex scrubs out her mouth with her fingers. She bends and tugs free a handful of dying grass, along with a crispy maple leaf, and shoves it in.

"What are you doing? Stop that."

She coughs, and I smack her on the back.

"Let's just leave, Molls."

"How? We have no car, remember? Besides, if we don't get the power off, the whole place might go up."

"Who cares? It's not our house."

"But they'll die. We can't let that happen. And our stuff's in there. Our computers. My memory stick."

"How many times do I have to tell you? Cloud-based back-up system."

"Will you shut up about that already? I told you, my netbook's ancient. All the syncing slows it to a freaking crawl."

"Okay, okay. Whatever. What the fuck are we even talking about?" I grab her hand. "The studio. We need to turn the power off and unwrap Jane."

We crunch up the hill through the fallen leaves toward the studio, a blazing beacon in the night. I take off in a run, because I suddenly need to see another human face. Another *non-insane* human face. Metal music guides us all the way.

"Hold up, Molly. I can't run."

But I don't listen. I reach the studio and throw open the door. "Oh no ..."

This *can't* be good.

"What now?" Alex shouts over the blaring death beat. "I can't take anymore."

"It could be paint, right? We shouldn't automatically assume it's something else."

"Of course. Let's not jump to conclusions. I mean, just because it's streaked and smeared all over the walls, furniture, and floor."

I shrug. "Maybe Haze is a messy painter. Like, that's her process."

Alex shoves a palm into my shoulder. "Go in and look."

I shove back. "*You* go. I went into the kitchen first."

"Fine." Alex pushes her long brown hair out of her face, squares her shoulders, and takes a step inside. "There, I went first. Now get over here." She grabs me and hooks her arm through mine. Together, we inch into the room.

I smack off the stereo as I pass, but the silence doesn't help.

"Haze?" Alex sobs.

Red blares at us from every surface, somehow harsher than the music we'd just nixed. "Molly, do you — Oh God."

A figure is sprawled on the floor behind the sofa.

I recognize the white chunk of hair, the tattoos.

"So, that *is* blood," I say.

If Ruthie's forearm was a mess, Haze is the super-duper-deluxe version. She's drenched.

"She was painting with it?" Alex says.

I get an eyeful of her canvas and grunt my affirmation.

"You think she's dead?"

I grunt again.

We stand there for Lord knows how long. Finally, Alex lays a hand on my shoulder. "We should go. Call 911."

"No." I grab her arm. "The power."

"I don't want to shut off the lights with a dead body in the room." "We have to," I say.

"But how will we call 911? The phones won't work." "Our cell phones?"

"Nancy said they don't get service out here."

Alex is right. My phone hasn't had any reliable bars this whole time. "What about the neighbors?"

"We're going to shut ourselves in here, in the dark, with a dead body?"

"Look." I grab Haze's phone from the coffee table. "It will give us enough light to get back with."

"Okay." Alex wipes the tears from her face and searches cabinets, then the closet. "Jackpot. Circuit box and storm supplies. Candles. Flashlight. You ready?"

I nod.

Alex flips all the switches, and we're plunged into darkness. "Wait a minute." I say. "We only have to do the ones for the basement in the main house. We're such dumbasses." "Excuse me if my brain doesn't work right after I eat *people*." "Well, technically, it was only one person."

"Not helping, Molly."

Click and the studio is ablaze again. Alex studies the box for a moment then re-flips two switches. "That should do it."

We race back to the house. I know we should do something about Ruthie, now passed out on the kitchen floor, but I blow by her and head to the basement. Alex trails behind.

Smoke from Jane already wafts up the stairs. My lights cut through the thick cloud, now suffused with a new smell—like charred bacon. "Oh, God. Alex, hurry."

We cough. My eyes burn and tear, but I open a window, and that helps some. The lump of stuff that is Jane still sits on the sofa, no part of her visible anymore through her self-inflicted cocoon.

And she's not moving.

"How the fuck did she do that?" Alex asks.

"Don't ask me."

"It's all melted and fused together," Alex says. "We need scissors or something."

"There's a pair in the knife block in the kitchen." "I'll go."

I keep at it as Alex stomps upstairs, but I make meager progress with fingers alone. "Jane? If you can hear me, make a noise or something." But there's no way she's alive in there. She can't be. Suffocated, probably.

I pull and twist and manage to uncover a patch of charred forehead. I'm across the room before you can say Jack Robinson. I no longer blame suffocation. I blame electrical burns.

"Alex. We're too late. Too late."

Why won't Alex come?

Silence from upstairs.

"Alex ...?" Tears choke off my voice.

My rubbery legs barely hold me. I trudge up the stairs on numb feet. "Alex, answer me!"

I try the kitchen first, but aside from Ruthie's prone form, it's empty.

Tap. Tap. Click.

I jump, immediately thinking of Jane and her knitting needles. No, that's not the sound of knitting needles. It's typing. "Oh no she *isn't*." Yes, she is.

"Alex, are you crazy? What the fuck are you doing?"

She's on the great-room chaise, laptop open, typing like a dervish. "I just had this thought, Molly-Doll. Wait one minute. I need to get this down before I forget." Her voice is *so* wrong.

"Alex, Haze is dead. I'm pretty sure Jane's dead. Ruthie may be dying. And you're ... *writing*?"

"I need *one* minute."

I've had enough. I have to get out of here. Now.

But a force in the hallway stops me dead in my tracks.

And where do you think you're going? The voice exudes glee, and she giggles. I want to smile and scream, both at the same time.

I'm frozen in place. My diaphragm locks up. I gasp, but still can't seem to get enough oxygen to my dizzy brain. Shakes ripple through my body. My leg muscles give up entirely. I collapse to the floor in a heap a second later.

Isn't that nice. I do like a compliment. Now, don't you want to let me in? Your friends did, and you see how much work they got done.

I try to speak, but my face is numb.

Come on, let me in, and I'll give you all the inspiration you could ever want.

A breeze kicks up. It surges to a gale that swallows up Alex's *tap-tap-tapping.*

I screw up my throat, strain every muscle in my face. My eyes bug, and something flares bright in my vision for a second, but I manage it. "NnnnNNO!"

The gale grows into a tornado. Gray gauze air spins and churns around me.

Oh, silly girl. There's no denying me. I merely asked to be polite. Your friends gave me enough strength to take what I want without permission. Even you.

And then there's nothing but laughter. Coming from my own personal cyclone and ringing in my head. I raise my trembling hands to my ears, but it does no good.

Not a laugh anymore. A mewling growl.

Louder and louder by the moment.

I add my scream, but it's washed out by the power of the demon's rage.

The pressure inside my head builds. Soon it will be too much for my puny skull to manage. Warm wet tickles my right hand. I remove it from my ear. It's smeared with blood. My blood.

The cyclone shoots away from me in a gray rush. It masses near the kitchen entryway. Pulsing. Beating. Writhing.

I can't tear away. I'm afraid to move. My noodle arms drop, and I pull my knees to my chest and rock back and forth on the floor, sobbing.

Grandpa John is there, in the hall, before me. His bird feather eyes regard me as he shakes his head. The rose-bloom of his cheeks and his stretching grin make mockery of the regret in his voice. "I told you, Molly-Dolls. But it's too late now, I'm afraid."

A huge *pop!*

The cloud whooshes at me. I open my sobbing mouth to gasp a lungful of air. With another laugh-growl, the cloud takes its chance. I never get the breath I was looking for. Instead, I swallow down...

The Muse.

Laughter all around me. Inside me. My vision goes gray, clouded by dank, dusty feathers.

But then, it doesn't matter anymore. Because now, I'm laughing too.

***

"Molly, I'm here," a man calls.

I know that voice, but it isn't important. My fingers fly over the keyboard. I don't even notice the pain anymore. But I let out a sob when I catch sight of the white nubs showing through the red at my fingertips.

Forget them. They don't matter. Nothing matters because I'm almost done. So close. A few more lines will do it.

"Oh my God. Molly? Molly! Are you okay? Where are you? Answer me!"

Feet pound their way to the great room. I flinch at the intrusion. "Molly."

He's on me now, but I don't care. I'm grinning and laughing.

Light as a feather.

He leans in close, hands fluttering near, but never quite touching me.

"Molls ... Oh God."

"Well, hi there, Derek."

"Oh God. What should I do?"

His milk face is funny, so I laugh.

"Help. I have to get help."

He paces and stabs his fingers at his cell. "Fuck your mother." He throws it across the room where it smashes against the wall. "The landline ..." He finds the handset, and the buttons beep three times.

"Operator? Please, we need an ambulance. There's been ... I don't know. An accident. At least three people."

He runs over to the chaise and slaps the face of the person who sits there.

I know her. "Hi, Alex!"

But Alex doesn't answer. She has feathers in her eyes, which seems strange to me, but I shrug and turn my attention back to my computer screen.

And I grin.

"I don't know," Derek says. "But please come. Please come." He's on his knees, staring at me and crying. *Crying!* Face all white and streaky. The voice coming out of the phone is small and shrill, but he's not listening to it anymore.

"What happened, Molly?"

"Huh?"

"What the hell's going on here?"

"I did it, Derek. I found my Muse. We all did."

He stares at me like he doesn't understand, like he can't see. I pick up my laptop and spin it around so he'll get why I'm smiling. He rips his eyes away from my face and squints to read it through the red smears: two little words.

Two *beautiful* little words...

The End.

Jessica Bayliss

Jessica Bayliss is an author of commercial fiction who loves nothing better than getting lost in a good story, whether in print or on film. She's soon to be published by Leap Books in "Beware the Little White Rabbit," an anthology of twisted YA stories inspired by "Alice in Wonderland" due out on April 14, 2015. She's currently collaborating with Three Worlds Press on a piece for their Sea Mist Series. Between short stories, she works on various novels, which span genres and age groups. Jessica has more books in her head than she knows what to do with and three completed novels she's currently querying. But woman cannot live on words alone. When not busy with her latest fiction project, she can be found loving her friends and family—especially husband, Eric— playing with one pesky Havanese, or trying to appease a particularly ornery cockatiel, typically with a cup of coffee near at hand. You can learn more about her at JessicaBaylissWrites.com

Birds and the Bees
Thomas Kleaton
#17216

LLACY SAT ON THE WEATHERED STEPS, watching bluebirds flit across the yard. School was out and Lacy, all of eight years old, was spending a few weeks at Grandma's house. She tousled her brownish-blond hair with her index finger as three crows vacated the power line across the street in a blur of flapping wings. Lacy loved crows and other birds, especially the pretty red ones that flew up onto the ledge beneath Stella's kitchen window to eat black sunflower seeds.

Snapdragons graced the sides of the steps. They exploded in pastel orange, yellow, and red-violet blooms, and the scent of Cape jasmine drifted on the air. Huge bees, yellow and black, scurried back and forth over the flowers, buzzing when they took off from one bloom and flew to another. Bees, bees, busy little bees, Lacy sang, tracing the outline of their flight with her finger. She remembered Tony, a boy in her second-grade class, who taught her how to catch the white-faced ones in her hand. She thought about her favorite book, Buzzy the Bumblebee.

"Lacy?" Stella, no more than five feet tall with grey hair cut stylishly short, stood at the screen door. "Why don't you come into the kitchen and have some ice cream?"

"Yay!" Lacy squealed, smoothing her Hello Kitty shirt with her hands. She tromped over the porch, letting the screen door wheeze shut behind her.

Lacy paused on her way back from the bathroom to examine the array of picture frames draped across her grandmother's antique dresser. There was her late grandfather, James, in his jungle fatigues from his days in Vietnam, smoking a cigarette while leaning on his rifle. A picture of her mother in high school, wearing a blue and orange cheerleader uniform. Pam's arms were parallel with her legs in a midair split, pom-poms blossoming from her hands. 1994 was emblazoned in gold in the lower corner. A photograph nestled at the rear caught her attention. She separated it from the others and strolled toward the kitchen with it.

Lacy plopped down in a chair and spooned some Blue Bell vanilla ice cream into her mouth, sliding the portrait across the table. "What's this, Grandma?"

Stella's hands were up, palms flattened out. Two black and white chickadees pecked away at the mound of seeds she held in each hand. She was smiling.

"Oh, that's from years ago, sweetie," said Stella. "I was really into feeding the birds back then. Your grandfather used to laugh at me so. Said I had a talent for attracting wildlife. A special talent." She pushed the picture frame back toward Lacy. "Now finish your ice cream, and you can go play in the yard for awhile."

"But I want to know about the birds," Lacy squirmed in her seat. "Okay, dear. You fill your hands with birdseed and stand perfectly still next to a bird feeder. If you're lucky, the birds will eat right out of your hands."

Lacy's eyes seemed to shimmer, pools of mocha. Her curiosity satisfied, Lacy stood up and placed her empty bowl and spoon in the sink.

"I think I'll go play now," said Lacy, sprinting toward the door with the vitality possessed only by eight-year-olds. She brushed by the screen door and down the steps in one fluid motion, leaving Stella to yell after her: "Watch out for snakes!"

***

Stella peered out the kitchen windows, watching as ominous dark grey clouds crept in from the west. A brisk breeze stirred the trees, and late-evening sunlight slanted through the breaks in the clouds, coating the room with a lustrous orange-yellow sheen.

Lacy's been out there awhile, she thought. Probably out back, playing in the blackberry brambles. She spotted the ancient garden shed, a small building with grey weathered oak planks and a rusty tin roof. A crescent had been cut into the upper portion of the door, which was ajar.

"Yoo hoo, Lacy, time to come in now," Stella hollered through the window. "You'd better not be in that nasty old shed."

Stella had set a German chocolate cake on the table and was pouring two glasses milk when the screen door into the kitchen scraped open.

Looking almost directly into the sinking orb of the sun, Stella watched Lacy step into the room. Lacy was a mere silhouette, the invading sunlight fashioning a crude corona around her luminous hair. Her tiny arms were outstretched, and Stella sensed tiny figures clambering over her head, giving Lacy the appearance of a serpent-haired Gorgon. Lacy, who would do anything to impress her grandmother.

"Grandma! Look what I did! Isn't it neat?" she said, a prim smile playing over her lips.

Fear seized Stella's heart with chilly fingers. She mumbled something as her hand went to her mouth, managing only a slight oog sound. She stumbled backwards into the table, knocking a glass of milk to the floor.

Lacy glided across an imaginary stage, listening to the clapping of the audience rise to a crescendo. A diadem of blackberry blooms encircled her hair, and a three-tier array of brambles and blooms formed a crude corsage pinned to her shirt by thorns. Blackberry vines twisted around her pants legs like ivy climbing a trellis. Several blooms were tangled in her shoelaces. She wore an old pair of faded gardening gloves, and a pair of rusty shears jutted from her pants pocket. She held a large Snapdragon bloom in each hand with the elegance of a queen preparing to knight someone with a gleaming sword.

Buzzing and crawling over the blooms were at least a dozen bumblebees.

"Don't move, Lacy." Stella scrambled under the sink for a can of flying insect killer. "Be perfectly still."

Bees were already cruising around in ever-increasing arcs, attracted by Stella's perfume. A bee veered toward Stella who, in her terror, began swatting empty air. She sprayed the flying insect killer in a circle in a futile attempt to disperse the bees. The pungent scent of bug spray permeated the kitchen. She imagined the bees fleeing from a giant can of Raid, just like in the commercials.

The hollow drone of humming wings filled Stella's ears as more bees circled her head. One hovered in front of her. She could clearly make out its black face. It landed on her chin. Another bee joining the foray landed on the soft skin of her neck and stung her. When she bleated in pain, yet another angry bee crawled over her teeth onto her tongue, stinging her again and again.

Stella collapsed into one of the chairs, her eyes watering, making a gagging sound as she choked on her own swollen tongue. Bees crawled over her lips like Blue Bottle Flies on road kill. Stella snatched her purse from the table, groping for her cell phone to dial 911. Another bee, furious, skipped over her eyebrows, stinging her across the forehead. She slipped in the spilled milk and heard a dry crack when her hip connected with the floor. The cell phone skittered across the linoleum. Her hands caressed her eyelids, which were already swelling shut.

Lacy stood crying in the center of the kitchen floor, bumblebees clamoring over her clothes. Her tear-streaked brown eyes drifted over her grandmother; her delicate features wrinkled in sorrow.

"I couldn't find any birdseed, Grandma. I couldn't find any birdseed..."

The End.

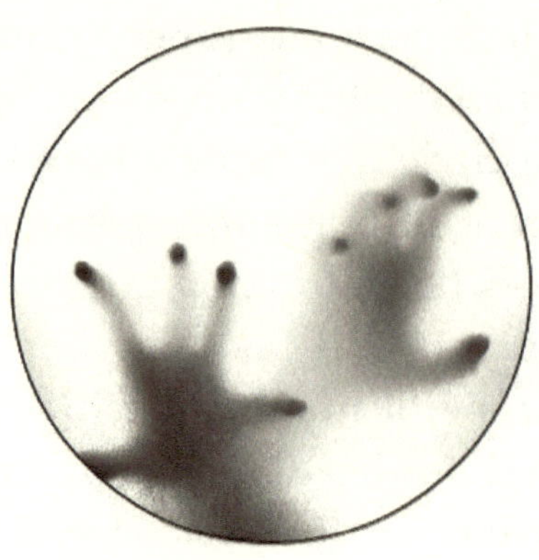

Thomas Kleaton

Thomas Kleaton is a freelance horror writer. His stories have appeared in Dark Eclipse Magazine, The Horror 'Zine, Spooky Halloween Drabbles 2014, and the paper anthologies Bones; Cellar Door: Words of Beauty, Tales of Terror; Serial Killers Tres Trias, The Horror 'Zine Summer 2014, and the special Halloween issue of Riding Light Review.

Dark Verse

S
The Thing That Goes
Bump In The Night
Ian Sputnik
Physician: Dr. Lotherton
8715-AED19
#93966

I am the reason ogres hide in their caves
Trolls under bridges and vampires in graves

I have the power to block out the sun
The means and the will to kill everyone

I reject reason, for no reason at all
My damnable actions are bound to appal

I am the darkness, a plague and a scourge
Mournfully solemn and a pitiful dirge

I am pure loathing, evil refined
But I am no Demon. Worse, I am mankind.

Ian Sputnik

Ian Sputnik is a writer of short form horror and dark verse. He resides in the UK with his wife. His debut piece 'The Darkness' was published by Sanitarium Magazine in issue 25.

S

Sleep Is Just An Open
Relationship With
Death

Layla Cummins

Physician: Dr. Lichten
6428-SED41

66567

Those watching wring their hands in mute
despair to know that life is fading from your
heart

and every time you close your eyes I'm
there. Hypnos and I work hand in glove
to bear the weight of your corroded
body part.
Those watching wring their hands in mute despair.

I fear the light and in the morning
glare, I shrink into the gloom that I
impart
but every time you close your eyes I'm there.

Our time from neither nap nor blink
feels fair and so I close the gap with my
dark art.

Those watching wring their hands in mute
despair To glimpse death's lovesick shadow
in the air above your bloodless brow, mere
threads apart, for every time you close your
eyes I'm there.

But theirs is not a love that can compare;
When daylight fades I know we'll soon
depart. Those watching wring their hands in
mute despair, for every time you close your
eyes, I'm there.

Layla Cummins

Layla Cummins is an author who has only recently dipped her toes into the unfamiliar waters of poetry writing. She grew up in Bristol, England and lives there with her family and three unruly cats that don't always get along. Her short fiction has been published in Bugs: Tales That Slither Creep & Crawl, 100 Doors To Madness and online at The Saturday Evening Post, with more anthologies in the works. She mans the 2nd Reads folder over at Grimdark Magazine and writes articles for the quarterly issues. Also an aspiring screenwriter and has put several screenplays-in-progress to one side whilst she concentrates on finishing her novel. Her first ever TV pilot was a finalist in the Sir Peter Ustinov Television Scriptwriting Award in 2014.

S
I Am No More
Austin Muratori
Physician: Dr. Edgar
9828-SJE41
#74078

The darkness swallows my wicked soul
As demons crawl in tortured silence
Making their way to me.

Teeth click in a chattered chaos
While another chuckles with glee.
Closer now evil creeps.

The darkness smells of rotting flesh.
As my dying corpse trembles
Eyes glow a vicious red.

Pain burns through my weak veins
Destroying my tattered core.
Time is up. I am no more.

Austin Muratori

Austin Muratori is a Writer, Filmmaker, Photographer, Musician and cancer survivor from a small town in Michigan. He is an avid reader who also happens to have an addiction to movies and junk food, especially Coca-Cola. He writes poetry, novels, short stories and screenplays of various genres his favorite being Horror/Suspense. Austin is constantly exploring new formats and genres in an effort to grow as a writer. As far as film goes Austin has been making films since he was 11 years old. Currently he is in his last year of film school at Full Sail University. He recently worked on a film titled "The End of the Tour" starring Jessie Eisenberg and Jason Segel and is due to be released in 2015. Another project he recently worked on is a feature horror film titled "Moorland" which premiered on October 20th 2014 with great success. It will be released on DVD and digital download in 2015! Feel free to check it out on Facebook: https://www.facebook.com/MoorlandtheMovie?ref=bookmarks

Austin is currently working on a few different projects. He is working on a short story called "Bleed" about a man who has an obsession with blood. He is also working on a short story and poem anthology along with a few different screenplays. There is a novel in the works as well. Follow Austin on Twitter @AustinMuratori Check out his website: https://austinmuratori.wordpress.com

On the.
Record

Congratulations on the release of Bird Box. How does it feel to be published?

Part relief, part cosmic gratitude, part unearthly, and part very real. I'd always imagined this moment coming, to the point of some big self-delusion, but when it came, when *Bird Box* got picked up, I sunk into a pool of astonishment and haven't got my whole self out of it yet. Which is probably good in some ways... but I think it's time to move on from the initial holy-shitness and really start to see it all as a career. Getting a book

deal isn't the finish line, of course, it's the day the "career" begins.

What started your interest in the horror genre?

My uncle introduced me to *Twilight Zone the Movie* when I was twelve or so and my love has been ballooning since then. My friend and I, we used to ask his grandmother if she'd rent *A Nightmare on Elm Street* for us and then after we watched it we'd ask her if she could go rent part 2. You know, in the same day. Then part 3. I'd sneak downstairs to watch the Saturday Shockers on television. I remember distinctly watching *Firestarter* that way, half scared of the movie but equally scared of Mom or Dad coming downstairs and hollering at me to turn it off. But the real affair began with the books. And 1985 was a helluva time to be a ten-year-old falling in love with scary books. The 80's were very good to me in that way. And whatever relationship I have with the genre, it's always been a slow, shadowy affair. As if I met a friend (or maybe just an entity) at a very young age, one nobody else knows about, and it's been around, hanging around, toying with me ever since.

Who are your favorite authors? Of the horror and non-horror variety?

I've been reading the new crop lately. John F.D. Taff. Stephen Graham Jones. J.D. Barker. These guys are wonderful, all in very different ways. Richard Thomas is doing things he might not even be aware of, as goes propelling the genre as an editor, putting out incredible compilations. Doug Murano and D Alexander Ward also, they're doing that, too. Ross E. Lockhart. Nikki Guerlain. Rena Mason. Lisa Morton. This new group is so colorful, so varied, that I can imagine a reader embarking upon their work and never even make it back to the 80's where, of course, the crazy boom went off. I love it all, I love em all, and maybe I'm "too open" to it, but the way I see it, even an Okay horror novel is better than most scary movies. Just open one up, any one, and you'll see what I mean. (I'm sure your readers already know this)

You mention that inspiration can be a devil in and of itself. If that's true, what gets you motivated to follow a story line?

When people talk about writing a book like it's running a marathon, I suspect they're referring to the holy-shit effort it takes to maintain the enthusiasm for the original idea. What I mean to say is; of course you love the idea or you wouldn't be feverishly writing a novel in the first place, and yet… your mind plays tricks… doubts… you know… just like anything else. At some point you start questioning shit, worrying that you've taken a great idea and accidentally dropped it in the toilet when you reached for something on the shelf. These are the moments that kill an author. That turn a potential author into someone who only wants to be an author. Because, if you want to be an artist, you've gotta finish works of art. With every book… there's a moment when you're in the deep end… it happens somewhere in the middle… maybe 37,000 words in… and you can't see shore on either side and you're worried you ate too many donuts and maybe you're not in good enough shape to swim all the way to the other side so you might as well quit and sink and drown and die that way. It's an awful idea; here you were fantasizing about strutting about town with your new book finished and instead they're gonna' find your bloated body washed up at Cedar Point. But there's a way through this; for me, it's not caring whether or not the book I'm working on is good or not. I'm not afraid to write a bad book and I think it's that Ed Woodian philosophy that carries me through most of what I do.

Then, once you've landed, once you're on shore again, you can fix as much or as little as you want to. But it's a helluva lot better to say "I can fix this; I can work with this draft" rather than "I don't know if I can write the book at all." So… to answer you directly… what motivates me is a pinch of guilt, and a lot of blind rolling downhill, not caring how good it is, but knowing that doing it is what has to be done.

It looks like creativity runs thick in your veins, as both an accomplished writer and singer/songwriter. Tell us about having your song become the theme for Shameless and how that's affected your career.

My band mates and I, we've been best friends since we were kids. They got into music before I did, I was writing, trying to write, and one day they invited me into the music world and asked if I could write songs. This led to a magnificent four years of living in New York City, touring the country for six more, and really it was a decade of self-discovery, cartoonish elation, some madness, and reinvention. All that said, don't go imagining rock stars or anything like that. If we played 2,000 shows, we played for 3,000 people… total. I'd like you to imagine delusional, broke boys who just didn't give a shit about "success" and truly experienced "the road." So, you can imagine our astonishment when Derek (drums) got a phone call that Showtime wanted to use one our songs as a theme song for a new show. It was magnificent news. And it still is. I wouldn't say it's "changed our career" in the way I suspect someone would ask that question (i.e. notoriety), but it gave us some much-needed money and, at the absolute very least it's given us something awesome to hold our head a bit higher about.

Is your band, the High Strung, touring? How do you balance both a career as a writer and a musician?

We're not touring right now because I more or less told the boys I wanna' write a new album, reinvent ourselves before we emerge from the swamp again. The problem with that is that I haven't written that new album yet, and I'm falling behind. Not that we have a hard deadline for anybody, but I can feel that I'm behind… in a spiritual sense. At the same time, what can I say? I'm working wonderfully hard on the next book, novellas, blurbs, and beyond. So, while I'm happy my life is comprised of 24/7 lunatic artistic endeavors… I do need to make room for the next album. I'm working on it.

Which is harder: writing music or writing fiction?

Ah, different animals, different appetites. I'd say neither are "hard" in that I'm in love with both. But, then again, love is hard I suppose. The good news about writing a song is that once my band mates get a hold of it, they can change an alright thing to a great thing by electrocuting it to life. With the book, you're out there on your own. And yet, that sounds like an advantage, too, in that there's nobody to be shy in front of, nobody to perform for until you're done and hand it to your publishing house, which of course is a kind of performance, too.

It seems like your book got sent over to Nelson almost by accident. Were you hoping to get the manuscript out there? How long had you been working at getting it published?

Well, I know what you mean when you say "by accident" but it wasn't exactly like that. What happened was, I'd been writing novels for years (and failing at writing novels for years before then) and the number of books was getting pretty high and I would post online about finishing this or that draft. *Wrapped up a rough draft today; anybody wanna' skydive later?* And a friend of mine from high school saw the posts and called me up, told me he'd been working with an entertainment lawyer… a literary lawyer no less… and would I mind if he sent the lawyer one of my books? I was all for it, though I wasn't sure where it would lead, you know… how could I be? The lawyer liked the book, called me, told me he had a great manager in mind. The managers called me (there were two of them then), said they'd like to represent me, and from there we shopped it to agencies. Kristin Nelson seemed like an odd choice only because her website stated she didn't work in horror, and yet Wayne (lawyer) and Ryan and Candace (managers) were right in sending it to her. So… "accident" only in that I didn't set out to meet the team myself… but no accident in that I'm a firm believer in the Theory of Momentum: if a man stays in motion, he may not end up where he envisioned himself landing, but he's gonna' end up somewhere new all the same. So, some may call it call it lucky even, the way this story panned out, but remember that before all this, I'd been writing alone for decades. That kinda' makes it a darker story, and that's the truth. As goes "working on getting it published," I'm not sure if it was because the band was touring and we were making just enough to scrape by, or if it was because I felt a sense of progress with the boys, traveling from city to city for so many years, but I never really tried to shop the rough drafts. That's not to say it was a hobby (gross word), I just never looked at the book with dollar signs in my eyes. I had brief run ins with people who might or might not help, that kind of thing, but it wasn't until the lawyer entered my life that it all began rolling.

Do you branch out into other modes or genres of writing? Do any others interest you that you have yet to explore?

Some of my friends and first readers tell me that I don't write horror at all. That these books are strange literary tales, *Bird Box* included. But I know better. Because I don't see the genre as only being vampires, wolves, and the undead. I love that trio, but I don't write about them, not yet. And so… rather than saying I don't write "horror," I argue that most people could benefit from expanding their definition of horror. It's a magnificent, infinite, life-changing genre… and I have no plan on turning my back on it. Feels like I was born here, live here. Horror is home.

Where did you grow up? How much did that influence your professional life?

I grew up in suburban Detroit and I think that the American suburbs in the 1980's were ripe as hell for stories, horror stories, real world tales. In fact, come to think of it, I'm not sure I've ever really considered just how much that upbringing has influenced my writing until right now, with your question, because it's bringing me to realize that the ideas that excite me the most are the ones that have something to do with the way I was brought up. I wonder; do all artists feel this way? They must, yeah? And at the same time, I've met artists who write of places they've never been, as if by writing about them they can travel there after all. But, yeah, yes, turns out the suburban upbringing has played a big part in all of this. Man, it was joyful, magical, dark at times, bizarre, and maybe it even acted as a palette of sorts… a canvas a city maybe couldn't be, not in the same way, ready to be written about, written upon.

What absolutely scares the living daylights out of you?

I'm at the psychic, right?, and she's reading my cards, my fortune, and while she's talking she slips me a piece of paper, keeps talking, as if nothing's happened. And as she goes on, I discreetly read the paper and it says, *There's been someone crouched beside you, staring at you this whole time. Possibly your whole life.*

You've been racking up award after award with Bird Box. Did you expect this sort of success with your first novel?

Ah, shit. Hmm. Well, I'll say this: I used to interview myself all the time. Walking around town, interviewing myself. I'd imagine a whole shelf at the bookstore of books I'd written. And I got so good at this thing that I became happy in there, that world I'd invented. And in that world there were awards, sure, and speeches, and discussions with imaginary editors and the works. So… I'm not sure how to answer this one because rather than "expect" this sort of thing to happen, I think I wrote a novel in my head in which it *did* happen. Asking me if I expected these awesome things to happen for *Bird Box* is almost like asking if I expect the events in *Bird Box* to happen, too. At some point, my reality and my fiction melded and I'm sure there's a doctor out there who has the right jaws of death to pry the two apart again, but I don't wanna' see him.

What's coming down the pike with you for writing? When can we expect a new release?

I'm a week or two away from submitting book 2 to HarperCollins. Already wrote her, now I'm rewriting her and then I gotta' read that rewrite one more time. Haha. Sounds like a wheel, eh? It's not a sequel to *Bird Box.* That would feel insane. And I don't exactly have a title for it yet or I'd tell you what it is.

What do you do outside of writing and singing? What's a hobby that you don't get to do very often, but is one of your favorites?

I run. I love going to the symphony. I love fishing with Mom. I'm not sure I have any hobbies, honestly. I understand that makes me sound severe, but the truth is, I spend almost all my time reading, writing, running these days and I'm so fucking glad I do. Because I spent years thinking I was getting more done than I was. You know what I mean? At some point, some when, the numbers of all of this became very clear to me and I fully understood that if I wanted to get all of these ideas on paper, I was going to have to fixate, almost maniacally. So I did. And so I am. And thank God.

What advice do you have for aspiring writers who think there's not enough time in the day to sit down and write? How did you find the time and what are some of your writing habits?

Well, the first thing, the very first thing, is that a man will do what he loves doing. He just will. We're all creatures of lust and desire and doing what we want to do when we can however we can. So… now the question becomes… "I know I'm a writer but I can't seem to finish this book! Why?" And the best answer I can give is, "Don't be afraid of tangents. Don't be afraid of writing a bad book. Don't get snagged on silly things like character names. Use your own as a place-holder. Don't be afraid to say no to plans… for weeks… months… until it's done. Get used to saying, 'Sorry, I can't hang tonight guys. I'm working on that book.' Say it until it's done. Then go out. And when you do, you're gonna' be the most charismatic version of yourself your friends have ever seen."

Thank you again Josh for taking time out to talk to us.

We hope you have enjoyed our time with Josh. If you would like to find out more, please head over to his Facebook page or follow him on Twitter.

A Little More about Josh:

Inspiration is a dangerous word. I think of it as its own monster; Inspiration. It's an inverse monster; instead of fearing its arrival, we wait for it, forever, whether or not it comes. In the meantime, nothing gets done. The best way I know of to defeat the Inspiration monster is to try and write every day, feeling good or not, and then, after reading through it all, seeing that the days when the monster was in the room were no better than the times he didn't show up.

Editor's update:- Since this interview was conducted and first published in 2015, Bird Box has been adapted into a major motion picture direct by Susanne Bier and starring Sandra Bullock.

<u>Congratulations Josh.</u>

Hello horror lover.

If you've been suffering from a persistent desire
for just a little more unpleasantness in your life,
we have the answer:

NOCTURNAL
TRANSMISSIONS

Nocturnal Transmissions is a fortnightly podcast featuring
inspired performances of dark tales both old and new
by voice artist Kristin Holland.

Find them at
nocturnaltransmissions.com.au
or wherever good podcasts are purveyed.

If you have any feedback or would like to leave a review please head over to Amazon and share your thoughts about Sanitarium.

Thank you for your time and we salute your love for all things horror.

https://www.facebook.com/SanitariumPublishing